I0818051

# Vehemence

A catalogue record for this book is available from the National Library of Australia

Cover design by Lizzacreative.

First Printing: MARCH 2025

Hardback ISBN: 978-1-7638145-1-6
eBook ISBN: 978-1-7638145-2-3

*There are none so blind as those who will not see.*

# Contents

LORIE BRINK

# Vehemence

An anthology of love,
anger and other emotions

# Gunnie's Last Round

Lorie Brink

# Gunnie's Last Round

## Lorie Brink

Lorie Brink

B&W image by Lorie Brink

# Contents

# Chapter One

Allowing the wave of grief to wash over me as I sat amongst the Rose Garden Memorial clutching at the old porcelain vase, I was also relieved I had deliberately waited until all the other mourners had ceremoniously opened their brightly coloured umbrellas, said their last goodbyes and disappeared into the low-lying grey cloud. I still wasn't sure if it were right for a man to cry in public. In between sobs and sniffles I talked to the man I never got to meet, yet got to know through my mother's memories. Now, my late mother's memories.

"My mother, your wife, together you shall be in Heaven, and here I sit all alone with memories and a lousy photograph of your wedding. I found mum clutching it as she rocked in your chair. She said you called out her name. Then she wept, held my hand and said I was to take you back to where you belonged. A place you always said was home and you had been away for far too long. I turned to look at your containment, Dad, this old porcelain vase sitting upon the polished mantelpiece, when I heard a soft sigh behind me. When I looked back at Mum, she was at peace and left me with a beautiful smile. So now, I guess you should both be together in the place where you called home."

I sobbed and felt something ruffle my hair and I sobbed some more.

Eventually, I stumbled back to the only home I had ever known. Mum had taught me from a young age that to get anywhere in life I had to work hard, be kind and respectful, and good things would eventually come my way. With that motto firmly entrenched, we managed to keep the wolves from the door. Her head for figures was useful to take on bookkeeping work and I had always loved two things. Comprehending earth science and sketching landscapes. The former is now my job, the latter is my hobby. My throat was sore and my eyes hurt, even my bad eye ached as I fumbled to close the front door behind me. I cradled Dad's containment with tenderness, except this time he stayed on the old vinyl topped dining table. I looked at the green cupboards in the kitchen, the clunky fridge that was older than my 28 years then at Mum's floral apron, neatly folded atop her recipe books. The tears fell and I just blindly stared into the surreal void.

As the shadows lengthened, the ringing telephone caught my attention. Lifting my aching head off my numb, folded arms, I groaned loudly and finally admitted I had out-grown the dining chairs from the 1950s. I eased upwards to my height of six foot two inches and stretched out both arms, easily picking up the phone receiver with one hand while opening the fridge door with the other.

"Hello?" I answered quietly, staring at the half full bottle of milk.

"Hello Toby, it's Lucy Smallwood. Today was a beautiful service for your dear mum..."

"Yeah, yeah it was. Um...thanks for all the organising you did, your amazing song and...well...thanks for...well...everything really. I'm glad you and mum were friends...the...the bright colours were a nice touch too. Mum would have loved that. Thank you."

"She was a remarkable woman, going through the pregnancy, having and raising a fine man like yourself on her own wasn't a small feat. She was very proud of you, Toby and about time you knew that you got the job on your own accord."

"Thanks, Mrs Smallwood. Um...the other day you mentioned something about a field trip...then..."

"Then your life changed drastically. Mine too. Young man, you need to take time to grieve and I'm older than your mum, so heed my advice please. We all grieve differently. I've had many losses during my sixty years and still have not found the best fit, but one thing that has been consistent is doing something I'm passionate about. You know how I love to sing?"

I chuckled softly. "Yes, I'll never forget the day I waited outside your office door as nervous as all heck with my single paged CV, and you were standing at the window singing to the world like you were on stage!"

"Exactly. I had returned from my favourite aunt's funeral and needed to get through the day. Back then, it wasn't easy for a woman to have her own business even if it was playing with rocks and stones, but it was my late husband's passion and I'd managed to keep his dream alive for five years. Then you entered my office and made my life a lot easier. Toby, that was ten years ago, to the day. We're still in business and we've kept his dream alive, now with a staff of nine and exploration grants! And I sang even louder when I got home today. It's a type of escapism for me."

I shook my head and thought how funny, but not funny, life can be.

"Hell of an anniversary, Mrs Smallwood. You're not going to fire me, are you?" I failed with my attempted humour and sniffed a bit too loudly.

"Good heavens, no! If you are up to having a work-oriented conversation over a home cooked meal this evening, I'll set a place for you at my table."

"Let's face it, I'm surrounded by mum's perfume, her presence in the kitchen is so prevalent, I'm...I don't know where to be."

"Your mum will always be where you are because she's in your heart. Talking and sharing memories will keep her alive. So...does six o'clock suit you?"

I wiped the big elephant tear away from my cheek and sobbed into the back of my hand, nodding my head. Swallowing hard and taking a deep breath, I replied, "Thank you, Mrs Smallwood, yes, I'll be there. What can I bring?"

She laughed. "You're a chip off the ol' block, lad. Just yourself and an appetite. See you then. Bye bye."

"Thank you and bye."

I am always pleasantly surprised how comfortable I feel in my boss's company. Mrs Smallwood, a pocket-rocket, hardworking, stoic woman of British descent can hold her own in negotiations around a boardroom table, as well as being the domestic goddess performing her magic in the kitchen. Her two sons were architect and construction bigwigs in the city and graced her with delightful daughters-in-law and grandchildren. To her boys, I am like a younger brother and when us three lads got together, we did what all men did. Hopped on our Harley's and cruised to our favourite waterhole. This lady and my mum had met many years ago at a Country Women's Association fund raising event for the Returned Servicemen's League. Their husbands had served and died for their country albeit decades apart.

With all traces of the delicious roast chicken and vegetable dinner cleaned up, Mrs Smallwood showed me her late husband's gem stone collection. He was a great fossicker and lapidarist. All that paled into insignificance when I held the clump of ironstone trying to disguise its quartz interior and the beautiful gold vein.

"And that, Toby, is why I would like to have a work-oriented conversation with you."

"Mrs Smallwood, I am all ears," I said with a watery grin and gently placed the gorgeously ugly rock back into her hands.

Her knowing smile and twinkling eyes confirmed my thoughts.

"Goodo, come sit in the lounge and we'll chat."

Ever since a little kid, I always sat on the leather ottoman and naturally took my seat. Mrs Smallwood sat in her favourite old faded rocker, typically put the ball of wool on her lap and started clicking the knitting needles. She could talk the hind leg off a donkey and kept you captivated with her story-telling and not once would she ever look down at whatever she was creating. When I got lost in the conversation, I'd try and work out if she was knitting socks or a scarf. Invariably I was horribly wrong, but this time I could tell she was knitting covers for clothes hangers. The bundle of wooden ones on the carpet by her feet gave it away.

"Toby, as I was saying, this field trip is going to take you across to South Australia and I want you to take your time. If you wouldn't mind going via Sydney and delivering a parcel to each of my sons on your way through? They've got something for you as well."

I frowned, rubbed it away and hoped they weren't big parcels because I really wanted to take my bike for a very long ride. I guessed it'd take me three weeks to do what was needed.

"For how long can I be away?"

"You've accumulated a lot of holidays and by rights, I owe you long service leave. I'm going to suggest four months."

"Four months? Mrs Smallwood, that's a very long time without pay!" I nearly fell off the ottoman in shock.

"You get paid to have time off, silly! What did you do with your pay all these years?"

I shrugged nonchalantly. "Just gave it to Mum. She did all the shopping, knew which bills had to be paid and when, I own my bike now, so she'd give me some to do with what I pleased."

"And?"

"Oh, saved some, spent some. I'm a man, Mrs Smallwood!"

"One that isn't stupid either. Now, Toby, your mother was a very organised woman..."

"Indeed, she was," I murmured, wondering where the conversation was heading.

I sat patiently and listened intently to her explaining how I would inherit the old family home including what was left of the mortgage, of which was manageable given the savings account I had unknowingly contributed to. To say I was gobsmacked would have been an understatement. I had owned my bike for one whole year and had babied it for the four years I'd been paying it off like it was my only possession, just entrusting my mum...well, being totally slack and expecting her to take care of the parental things actually. I hung my head in shame.

"Don't be too harsh on yourself, Toby. As you said, you're a man. A twenty-eight-year-old man who for the last year or so has looked after his ailing mother and has just been smacked in the face with reality. You have been given the opportunity to better yourself with the ways of the world and grow up rapidly. Cooking, reading the earth and sketching aren't your only strong suits you know. Now, I have a niece who is looking for a rental for several months. She's poorly in health and will have her Church people around for help."

I looked at her blankly.

Mrs Smallwood tutted and sighed. "Let's have a cuppa."

I obediently got up and put on a brew, all the while my head was spinning. Opportunity to better myself? I may have lived at home but I wasn't a Nancy Boy. Far from it in fact. Rent out our home? A stranger? Church people? Delivery boy to the concrete jungle? Immediately I thought of dad. What would he do? That's when I smiled because according to mum, whenever he was faced with a multitude of tasks, he'd jump on a horse and go do what had to be done. I didn't have a horse.

"Mrs Smallwood, four months you say?" I asked gently as I placed her delicate tea cup and saucer on the even more delicate crocheted doily on the little side table.

"Yes."

"Tell me more about the work-oriented component of this conversation please."

The way this woman's eyes twinkled when she knew she had gotten her way always made me smile broadly. I watched as she took a dainty sip of the tea, sighed happily and gently replaced the cup with its melodic 'tink' on the Fine Bone China saucer. When Mrs Smallwood puts down her knitting, it is time to pay serious attention to what she was about to tell you.

Essentially, I was to pick up a document from her sons that would allow me to prospect for a gold-bearing reef, somewhere north of Yunta in South Australia. Whether I did the fossicking on my way to taking my folks home or on the way back to my home, was entirely up to me. In the meantime, her niece, Abigail, could rent the sunroom which adjoined the verandah. In order for that to work, all I had to do was give it a lick of paint, replace a couple of louvres, strengthen up the railings and secure the floorboards.

"How long did you and Mum have this planned out?"

"We talked about it at the CWA Christmas fete, then we..."

"Landed those massive exploration projects in January and May which we've only just finished. Mrs Smallwood, it's already September and you haven't had a holiday either I might add."

"Don't you worry about me, young man, this house will be full of little feet and noisy mothers soon enough. You could be quite the popular one if you cared to stay?"

I laughed out aloud and stood up. "I wasn't sure I needed an incentive, but now I am definitely not going to hang around. I will get cracking on the sunroom for your niece."

After thanking my lovely aged hostess for her hospitality and support, I felt a tonne lighter after being given a shove. By the time I got home, I knew exactly what I was going to do...even if the old biddies had been scheming for so long, I found it hard to believe mum would have wanted to die so young.

# Chapter Two

I cried myself to sleep and dreamt of my father on a horse, riding into the sunset with a massive broom sweeping away his trail. It was the face in the clouds that made me awaken with a start. Mum! I got up and immediately went into her bedroom and sat on the edge of her bed. I knew the suitcase underneath it held all her memories...what I couldn't work out was why dad would have covered his tracks.

Sitting at the dining table with the photographs and old letters piled up around Dad's containment, there weren't any pictures of his horse or any horses for that matter. That was until I opened a small yellowed envelope containing one photograph. A little boy on a rocking horse being supported by an older, very tall man with very broad shoulders and a barrel-chest. I flipped it over to read, G'father, Cleve SA 190? written in unfamiliar handwriting.

I automatically guessed it was my father on the horse, and I shivered when I used the magnifying glass on the man. I was almost looking into a mirror. The chiselled nose and jawbone, the shoulders, barrel-chest and the height. It could have been me, except I had been graced with my mother's dark hair, brandy-gold eyes and dimples. Not the fair hair and presumably penetrating blue eyes of how dad had always been described.

I wouldn't know any different. All the photos were black and white and their wedding photo had been damaged with time.

I reached for their photo and stared. Even with the magnifying glass, it wasn't clear if dad had fair hair or any at all. He was a very tall man, very similar build to the man standing beside the boy on the horse which I had also inherited. All that was obvious. I looked at my dad again. He looked older than mum. I had never noticed it before. I opened my sketchpad and on the inside cover wrote down the dates I had grown up believing and now, in my saddest moment, doubting.

Date: September 1975 - mum passed away (aged 57) September 1947 – dad passed away (aged 29?) Feb 1948 - I was born.

I turned the rocking horse photograph over again and stared at the date. So, who was hanging on with wide eyes? Couldn't have been my dad, he wasn't even thought of. Mum never mentioned a brother or uncles or any other relatives and I was led to believe that both my folks were born in 1918. Mum appeared to know very little of my dad's parents, but had told me her and dad married hurriedly in May and sadly he died during the war when he was 29. I never asked which War. Rubbing my eyes, I reached for the set of encyclopedias containing the maps of Australia and learnt what I could about Cleve. I moaned out aloud. Sheep and wheat. Together, that meant a tonne of flies. The only consolation being the place was on the right side of the Spencer Gulf to where I had to take my dad, but a fairly long way from Yunta and almost half a country away from Lismore.

I then tried to find information about Australia's military history post World War II given dad's death was two years after it had ceased. There was only the British Commonwealth Occupation Force (BCOF) between 1945-52. I sighed heavily, I doubted if I would ever learn the truth and gave in to the knowledge that my dad died serving for his country, before I was born.

Two weeks later, both my parents' ashes were secured together and well-padded in the left-side leather saddlebag. To balance the load were the two brown-paper wrapped parcels tied with string for Mrs Smallwood's sons. My swag and kit always took up the pillion's seat, just like work always took up my time. I didn't realise I was lonely. Until now. Sure, I had a girlfriend, but...it was for mutual conveniences only. The town's gene pool was too small for my liking. 'A late bloomer,' my mother had called me. I had always replied, 'just protecting my heart.' And now, I'm heading to the unknown. I did a dignified wave to Mrs Smallwood and before I slipped on my open-face helmet, I gazed towards the Heavens and said a little prayer. As I said, Amen, I kick started my Harley-Davidson FLH Shovelhead. Its distinctive note was music to my ears.

After a full day's ride, sore butt, stiff shoulders and bug-splatted face, I rolled into the nominated watering hole and pulled alongside two other familiar Shovelheads. It was going to be a late night by the sound of the boys in the bar.

Three days later with a few additions to my riding gear including new sunglasses and a balaclava, I looked like a real threat on the road. Women turned their heads away, their men tried to make themselves look bigger behind the wheel as I blasted past, children either stared or ducked down, but the young chicks didn't have a care in the world and far too many were hitching rides in the back-blocks of New South Wales. I didn't want to think of the fourteen hundred kilometres ahead of me, nor the three days of riding which could stretch to four or five if I found a decent place that wasn't afraid of a six-foot giant on a Shovelhead. One with no tattoo, one good eye, no idea of anything outside of the State and who preferred to avoid confrontation.

Finally, the South Australian border! It was easy to do a quick tour of Yunta. Just one road straight through the guts of the dusty place and I kept on going. The drastic change of scenery captivated my artist's eye which almost begged me to stop and sketch, however, I felt compelled to continue with the ride.

Yet it was under a cloudless and vibrant sky where the sea of yellow canola flowers in full bloom surrounded by endless paddocks of green wheat had me mesmerised. Enough so, I pulled off the main road where my attention was also drawn downwards to the delicate but hardy wildflowers peppered along the rubbly dirt track. I automatically began sketching these seasonal native flowers in charcoal. Further into the scrub and noticing discolouration on the smaller rocky outcrops, I recognised the soil as red sandy loam with traces of clay. Atop a boulder with its 360-degree views, the spectacularly colourful landscape took my breath away. Shielding my eyes from the late afternoon sun, I could make out the silhouetted silos on the outskirts of a town. Reluctantly leaving this new-found Zen, I kicked my Harley alive, turned back onto the bitumen and admitted the change of scenery increased my excitement which brought about onslaughts of sugar cravings.

Acting like a magnet, the golden ball reeled me in. When the sudden transition of broadacre crops with isolated homesteads dotted across the countryside changed to stone houses on one side of the road and mallee scrub on the other; I was spellbound. The gleaming white Town Clock stood proudly in the middle of the wide main street. Above it, featured a prominent carving of a Fallen Soldier emblazoned on a poppy, haloed in the afternoon sun. A tasteful mural of the sheep and wheat pioneers adorned the structure's base along with the dates of all the earlier wars; the formation served as a Memorial.

The town's architecture was from a bygone era, which straddled a train line as it grew. A single church had the time-stamped construction of incredible stonework and amazingly, a bell tower. Attached to it in a grand engineering feat was a sizeable hall suitable for a large congregation, dance or town meeting. The blending of stone, red brick and timber was exceptional. The purple carpet of flowers from the ancient Jacaranda trees peacefully adorned the cemetery. I looked at the saddlebag containing my parents' ashes and smiled sadly. It didn't quite feel right. I went back to the Fallen Soldier Memorial and studied the dates chiselled around the structure. If dad died in 1947; where, in which war and how? All these questions rattled around in my head and nothing made sense and I was not about to question mum's information. Aside from that being impossible, it didn't serve any purpose now, but it was a mystery.

Modern day businesses shrouded in the historical hand-formed stone facades clearly indicated that history played an important role here. I felt I had stepped back in time when I saw an old textile factory which sensibly housed the museum. The traditional style businesses strategically placed along the main street was living history. This included the bakery proudly displaying its freshly made apple turnovers with Chantilly cream. Consequently, two were rapidly devoured. Anybody would feel as if time slowed down here. It was easy to describe the town as having a relaxed pace. Even the flies. They never left your face in a hurry.

The cleanliness of the town reflected obvious pride. Golden Wattle trees framed dirt compacted side streets, conjuring up images of horse-drawn carts laden with wool bales and bushel bags. An overwhelming sensation of nostalgia caused me to take a deep, steadying breath. Why did I feel so calm?

The local watering hole beckoned. A typical design for a typical two-level country pub, with a row of narrow windows positioned above and across the western facing entrance. Nothing else out of the ordinary. Bushel-brown painted exterior, rooms upstairs, horse rails out the front. As I pushed through the old-fashioned timber swinging doors, the Victualler looked up and extended a warm greeting. A quick surveillance of the naturally-lit, timber panelled room revealed that all hats were either on the floor or balanced on the knee. In one smooth motion I politely replied, stuffed the balaclava into my open-face helmet and left it on the floor in front of a stool facing the bar. I extended a friendly nod to those that caught my good eye and ordered a pint of Lager.

Quite high up the wall behind the bar, an impressive copper embossed panel replicated the same pioneering mural I saw on the Town Clock. Leaving a $10.00 note on the well-worn beer mat, I strolled casually towards an inwards swinging door marked 'Rams'. Complete with grubby face, messy hair and artist's bag casually slung across my broad chest, I quietly whistled a happy tune. Affixed to a mahogany wall, I caught my scruffy reflection in a mirror.

This extraordinarily large mirror was in the shape of a wheat bag inside a frame, which appeared to be covered in wool. I felt compelled to investigate further. The closer I got to it; the more a golden light beamed across my reflection. I slowly turned and stood in awe. The late afternoon sun streamed through those high glass panes and breathed life into the copper magnificence.

"The dead has risen," a gruff voice called out from a darkened corner.

"No, Sir, I'm as alive as you are," I replied respectfully, dipped my head and pushed through the door to the Gents.

Trying not to overthink the peculiar greeting, I cleaned myself up and recalled the history of the town and surrounding areas. It was famed for sending most of its men to war when the upper echelon finally decided that no more lives were to be lost from this community. There must be a lot of shellshocked old timers here, I thought. Best behave appropriately.

As I strolled casually to the bar, the schooner of golden ale gleamed like a tiny pot of gold. I downed it in one go, tapped the glass and grinned. "Please, Sir, may I have another?"

The Victualler roared with laughter and studied me closely. "Where you from, sonny?" and motioned for the bartender to pull another beer.

"The east coast where the schooner is almost double the size. All the same, can I have a room for several nights please?"

"Sure. We do meals and its extra for the bathrooms. We're a respectable pub, no floozies but upper-class escorts are tolerated, provided you keep the noise down."

"I'm not here to cause trouble, I just need somewhere to rest my aching bones. I've been riding for days."

"Horse?" the same gruff voice from the corner begged the question.

"Horsepower, Sir. Can I get you one?"

"Yeah, you can. I reckon you owe me more than one, Tobias Otto Gutterman."

I froze. I had never ever been called by my full name, not even when I was in trouble and mum in her sentimental ways had named me as per my father.

"Esquire. Tobias Otto Gutterman, Esquire, Sir, however I prefer to go by the name of Toby."

"You a lawyer?"

"No, Sir, an orphan."

I took both beers and approached the muttering to be greeted with a table being knocked over. An older man in his haste to get up sent it and several empty glasses flying.

"Hey, hey, easy, Gunnie."

The Victualler came rushing over and steadied the feisty old fella, firmly encouraging him to retake his seat.

Retreating out of harm's way, I took up residency at the bar and drank both beers swiftly. An older barmaid stepped in and pulled several more beers, taking one to the corner of the bar and putting mine in front of me.

"Thanks, I'll pay for his two. Cheers."

"He's not well in the head. What are you doing here?" she hissed.

Taken aback, I considered my reply before announcing quite loudly.

"Minding my own business in a town of strangers where it appears my name has history, of which I know nothing about. I am en route to take my parents' ashes to their final resting place."

I downed my beer, grabbed my helmet, nodded to whoever was paying attention and strode out with my head held high. As I straddled my bike, a deeply buried indescribable emotion bubbled to the surface. No. I don't like unfinished business. I could not leave without knowing how this old man recognised my father. So, I unclipped my kit and saddlebags, slung them over my shoulder and strolled back into the bar.

"I'll pay for the accommodation and bathroom, thank you, if you could tell me where to go...politely."

Again, the Victualler burst out laughing. "This way, sonny."

At the opposite end of the bar, he explained that Gunnie was a Veteran from several wars with vivid memories of yesteryear and vague memories of current days, therefore probably wouldn't recall his outburst.

"But he knew my name. I have never stepped foot in this State and sadly, I never knew my father."

"Well, mate, clearly there's history that needs sorting out. I'm going to stick around, best you do too."

"Not for long, I've got places to be and things to do."

This time, the Victualler paled and didn't laugh. "You are your father, Toby. By God, you are your father."

"Who was he?" I pleaded.

"One hell of a horseman...you obviously got your mamma's eyes and dimples...now, you're in Room Seven with your own bathroom. Freshen up, neat attire, dinner is served between six and eight. Bar closes at eleven. The old boy leaves just before we close."

With that, he slid a room key towards me, stared into my eyes and politely nodded his head. "Off you go, Toby, off you go."

# Chapter Three

Dinner was a very quiet affair with me enjoying my own company, several old photographs and a mighty fine lamb chop. Afterwards, a few lads challenged me to several games of pool which is damn difficult with one good eye, but thankfully I did sink a couple of balls even though I lost all the games. Good sports. Nearing nine o'clock, with a bit of Dutch courage under my belt, I approached the grumpy old man.

"Finely grew a spine?" he growled.

"Yes sirree," I replied lightheartedly. "Mind if I show you some photographs, old man?"

He grunted and slapped the table. I spread three of the five in front of him and he tapped the table like I was a bloody croupier. Of all the photographs, he picked up the one with the little boy on the rocking horse.

"Bloody things," he muttered. "Was surprised you wasn't killed earlier the way you used to jump on these bloody things."

"Who is on the horse?" I asked quietly.

"Sure isn't you on that damned thing, you fool. That's me, trying not to be scared."

"Scared? Why?"

I had to keep reminding myself that Gunnie was talking to me like I was my father.

After an extended coughing fit, he almost squeaked when he spoke. "Everyone was terrified of your father. My Godfather. That man right there. He was a giant in our eyes, but when he got real mean, his bad eye bulged. Hell of a way to go but, blown to bits mucking around with dynamite digging for gold. Dammed fool took me grandpappy and pa with him."

"Is that why you're angry with me?"

"You were a chicken-livered, yellow belly scrap of a boy, not as mean as your pappy but dammit, what's the go with the bung eyes?"

"No idea," I said and bit back a laugh.

"Yep, always the wise-arse."

"So, what happened?"

"You never showed up to school after the funeral, your mamma taught you from home while you was running the farm. Then years later, we was young men by then, one night, you come tearing down the main street riding this damned wild horse bareback like some injun. Hootin' an' hollerin' and got bucked off as an Army jeep cut a corner."

Old Gunnie had another coughing fit, laughed some, cried a bit and drank five more beers before he spoke again.

"I saved your sorry arse, then after breaking plenty of hearts, you go and fall in love with my girl and left without saying goodbye. Your momma got buried next to the Cross for your old man, who's buried beside my pappy's Cross and my mammy. You any idea where?"

"No, Sir..."

"Stop calling me Sir, you stupid bastard. Right here, you damned fool. This bloody place and you're late. You missed the ANZAC Day Parade.

Why, after all these years have you come back? Too late to talk to your momma, almost too late to talk to me. I ain't long for this earth, Tobias and not sure how I feel about seeing you all young and sprightly even and still with the bung eye. You sure done some growing. I done thought you got killed in the war. Then I heard you moved east with the nurse, got married and well, blow me down here you are."

He started rambling incoherently with the occasional clear word, usually a profanity, punctuating the confusing conversation. I tried as best I could to comprehend the history lesson and pick up any information that could be useful. Then Gunnie suddenly gripped my hand.

"We're not from here, Tobias. Our home is two hundred miles away. I don't want be buried here. I never even wanted my parents to be buried here, but I had nobody to bounce off. Sissie got swept up with the uniform love and life and left before I got back. She's long gone and I ask you, why the hell am I still alive? Ol' Bluey saved my sorry arse and kept me sane by letting me caretake the gardens around his pub. Those vegetables you ate? I grew them."

"Could tell they were freshly harvested. You've never been back home?"

"Ye deaf or somethin'? And I ain't getting on no bloody horse, Tobias."

"What about a motorbike?"

"Eh?"

That was the first time he looked at me like he saw me for the young man I was and not the ghost he thought.

"A Harley-Davidson," I said proudly.

Then the incoherent ramblings began again, and Bluey, the Victualler called 'last drinks' made his way over to Gunnie and helped him out of his seat.

"Can I help, Sir?" I asked politely as I stood up.

"Yes. Take your photos and go to bed. You and I will catch up in the morn."

Completely bewildered, I collapsed onto the well-worn old bed and fell into a dreamless sleep. Well, it was initially. Again, Mum's face in the cloud woke me but this time the cloud was casting a shadow over the jacarandas in the cemetery. It was five o'clock in the morning. I would never get back to sleep. Slipping the photographs into their envelope which stood beside my parent's urns, I slung the saddlebags over my shoulder and went for a walk through the sleepy town. The waft of freshly baked bread drew me like a moth to a flame and picked at the delicious warm loaf as I strolled towards the outskirts. My feet took me to the cemetery, my heart was already there, but my head was full of questions. The biggest one I regret never asking my mum was what the hell happened to my eye? Clearly, it's a hereditary thing and I definitely didn't want it to bulge! Way too freaky for me.

In the distance, a solo figure wrapped in a trench coat had just stood up from a marked grave and remained with a bowed head. I respected his or her privacy and went in search of my grandparents. The oldest part of the cemetery teemed with Crosses and headstones and going by Gunnie's explanation, that's where I would find some answers.

Morbid curiosity got the better of me as I read the names and dates of death on all the gravesites and put together the sad and sorry tale of the pioneers, the diseases, the babies and small children, the entire family plots and the rows and rows of soldiers who died in the Wars.

By the time I located my grandparents' final resting place, my heart was in my throat. I could almost hear the agonising wails of sorrow being cast to the wind. I read my grandmother's headstone, traced the outline on my grandfather's cross and sat heavily on the ground in front of it. September seemed to be a very sad month in the Gutterman family. I placed my parents' urns on the grass, swivelled around and laid back with them either side of my head.

"A bit of help would be nice, Mum and Dad," I said as I gazed up through the jacaranda leaves.

"Ask away," a voice called behind my head.

I was on my feet in a flash, gasping for air when I saw Bluey step around from several rose bushes. He was wearing the trench coat, and a broad grin.

"Morning, Sir! You scared the living daylights out of me."

"Don't you be getting too comfortable there, Toby, you've got years ahead of you. Walk with me, your folks will be quite fine here for a while. We'll collect them on the way back, I swear it."

Bluey filled in a few gaps of my youthful father's antics with horses and his uncanny knack of breaking hearts in a small town. The angry barmaid being one of them. She was devastated when he up and left in pursuit of the nurse with the dimples and dark hair.

"My mum never mentioned being a nurse or anything about a nurse."

"She wasn't, but her twin sister was. Your father was playing the field including my sisters. Your mum was recruiting women to join in the war efforts and as far as I know, the only one who fell pregnant. That's why he up and left. I only learnt all this years afterwards. . .he did the right thing and married his pregnant bride, went on a tour of duty and his platoon got blown to bits. Or so the story goes. Back in those days, any pretty girl travelling through was fair game. We knew it, they knew it and we all looked handsome in our uniforms. The Wars almost decimated the population in this area, hence the size of the cemetery."

I let the news hit me like a rock and numbly walked beside Bluey listening to his version of the history lesson. Something wasn't sitting right with the dates I knew of, including the one on the particular photograph.

"Sir, I was led to believe my folks were born in 1918, but the photo of Gunnie on the horse was dated nineteen hundred and a question mark. I just presumed they were the same age. Am I missing something?"

"They were the same age, Gunnie and your father that is. We all lied about our ages and many got accepted anyway because that was what was expected. Serve and fight for our country. This year's ANZAC Day Parade was the largest we've had for a while. The surrounding communities converged on us wanting to put the records straight. Suspect the Vietnam War had something to do with it. Anyway, not all the fallen called this town home. Your father and Gunnie included. Their own towns have no physical recognition or Remembrance Wall indicating their birthplace. So many young men, brothers, uncles, fathers, fathers-to-be and just plain simple farming folk, entire families and bloodlines were lost. Dying cruel deaths on foreign soil. For years to come, there will be many a fallen soldier returned to his home, you mark my words, Toby. May explain why you were never conscripted for 'Nam."

"Mum told me to take Dad home moments before she died," I blurted out.

"I am sorry for your loss, Toby, but by God you are practically a spitting image of your father and the last image many of us have of him."

"I'm twenty-eight, Sir. An orphan with a hell of a lot of questions."

"You won't get all the answers you seek. I'm telling you that right now. But it's only right that you know your father and Gunnie were born in 1898. Regardless, the advice I have for you is to make peace with Gunnie when he's mentally back in the day which is nearly all the time, fulfil your quest and go home."

"In other words, leave sleeping dogs lie?"

"Yep, pretty much. The dates, which War, the where and how your father died, the age discrepancy...none of it is going to change who you are."

I let that profound statement sink in, then asked, "Do you think he'd manage a bike ride?"

"As long as the old boy doesn't fall off."

"How come you're not as old as he and the other barflies?"

"I was only eight when the lads signed up. The youngest of nine by eleven years and the only one alive. Suppose I grew up wanting to be like them, our families were very close by the time I came along."

"I am sorry, Sir. That's a huge amount of sorrow."

I looked at him gazing to where he had stood amongst the greying headstones.

"Yeah, thanks. That whole row. My entire family. Gone."

I lowered my head and breathed out slowly. I did not know what to say.

"There are a lot of sour folks with bad memories in this here quaint town, and whilst the strangers flock to pay their respects and sample our produce, the living is left to deal with their own demons. These are swiftly buried when a fresh face is in town. Usually."

"Then along came Tobias Otto Gutterman, Esquire and ripped open the scars."

"That's what we call unintentional interference."

"Really?"

"You aren't the first and you won't be the last, Toby but even I did a double take when you walked in my bar. Now, let's go and collect your folk and thank the Good Lord you don't have your grandfather's ire. He was meaner than your father."

"You knew him?"

"His reputation will be around a lot longer than you and I if the stories get passed on. On your way out, get Gunnie to take you to the memorial site. It mightn't be pretty, but let him grieve. Seems September is an awfully sad month for a lot of our families."

On the way back to the pub, I had an epiphany.

"Sir, any idea where I can get a sidecar from?"

Bluey slapped me on my back. "I most certainly do. Come on lad, we'll get the old boys together and play in the shed behind the pub. You just might make a few of them smile and remember you kindly."

I blew a soft raspberry. "Man, I hope so. Mind if we stay in touch?"

"I'd like that very much. Say, what do you do for a crust anyway?"

"Geology, will be stopping at Yunta on my way back to do some fossicking."

He laughed loudly. "Stay away from bloody dynamite then. Don't need that to be hereditary too!"

# Chapter Four

Before the pub opened six days later with an ex-Army dark green sidecar affixed to my black Harley-Davidson, Bluey strode over and sat astride her while several of the other men encouraged Gunnie out from the pub. He'd been sprung several times peeping through thc curtains but we all pretended not to notice him. He appeared to be disinterested but his twitching lips was the dead giveaway.

"I hate horses," he stated loudly, "And bloody shovels! What is it with you Gutterman blokes?"

"You know your motorbikes!" I said totally astonished.

"Been around longer than you, boy," he growled.

Bluey intervened and beckoned him towards the contraption. "Come on, mate! See if you can get your sorry arse in this. You're going for a ride."

"I ain't!"

His six buddies told him categorically that he was, swept him off his feet and made him sit inside the sidecar. While he was adjusting his stature, Bluey popped an old open face helmet on his head and handed him a scarf.

"Tie this on, mate, we're going for a cruise."

I just stared, still trying not to show my horror. Nobody else had ever sat on my bike, let alone taken her for a ride. My heart beat rapidly and my breath shortened.

"Hey, Toby, what's your favourite snack from the bakery?" Bluey called out.

"Apple turnovers..."

He rolled his eyes and shook his head. His loud laughter was drowned out by the rumbling engine as he slowly navigated his way around the pub. They had quite the audience by the time they got out the front, all whistling and throwing their hats into the air. I felt a sense of achievement. I was doing the right thing.

The farewell just before lunch was quite an emotional event for all and sundry. Bluey pulled me aside and handed me a piece of paper. Afterwards, my handshake with him was the firmest one I could muster, as was his. We were both flexing our hands and smirking afterwards. Gunnie was in his element and grinning from ear-to-ear. I was about to kickstart my girl when he put up his hand.

In a loud voice he said, "Wait, Esquire. Mates, if I don't come back, know that I thank you from the bottom of my heart and don't blame the kid. But if I do come back, that's when you can blame him. Now, boy, kick this horse in the guts and let's get going."

I did as I was told and followed his hand signals to our first destination. My God! Even after all the years, it sure was a hole in the ground. I couldn't help myself and scoured the area for its tell-tale history.

"It was the only way to see what was beneath the earth," Gunnie explained clearly. "The old timers had found traces of gold but as it turned out, it wasn't here. You need to go further west or north, Esquire, just don't use bloody dynamite. Come on, I've said my piece. Let's go home."

I looked down frequently to see if the old boy was still breathing and thanked the Good Lord each time. I'd never known anybody to nod off in a sidecar but Gunnie showed it was possible. I firmly squeezed his shoulder as we rounded a sweeping corner that led into a sparsely populated old town. Again, I had my breath taken away as I slowed to a stop. The fields of lavender between the canola and wheat were stupefying. On the low green grassy rolling hills, clumps of white stood out like clouds against a plain sky. The flock of sheep were extensive. The vista was living art. I retrieved my sketchpad and charcoal and swiftly filled in the pages. Gunnie's snuffling snore broke my concentration and I nearly cried. He looked so old. The oldest person I had ever known and deep down he was as lonely as me. Plus, he was the only connection to my father.

I captured his character sitting in that sidecar with every ounce of respect possible. The blending technique inadvertently put a halo around him like the sun shining around the Fallen Soldier Memorial. I modified his helmet into a Slouch Hat and sketched the Rising Sun emblem onto the side. I had to include his nickname somehow. Gunnie was a Machine Gunner. I smudged the sidecar outline and had him profiled behind a Bren Gun.

"Stop staring at me, Tobias, it's creepy."

I played along even though his eyes were closed. "At least I know you're still breathing, Gunnie."

Then suddenly he gasped.

"Mate, can you get me out? I can't feel my legs." His voice was on the verge of panic.

I dropped my notepad and rushed over to him. Standing behind, I slipped my arms under his.

I spoke firmly, "On three, let me lift you. Ready?"

"You stupid old bastard, it was always on one. We never had time to count to three."

I didn't hesitate.

"On one. One."

As soon as his legs were visible, I scooped him out and stood him up, held him while I walked around until I faced him and steadied him until he shrugged free.

"I'm good. You dropped something. Hurry. We need to get out of here. They're coming."

The whole time he was talking, his eyes were still shut but rapidly moving under his eyelids.

"Dammit Tobias, get away from there. Come here and duck down. Don't get in their road, they're bloody wild. Your father will have our guts for garters! Dammit Tobias. Grab that trunk. I don't want to see that bloody ugly eye."

"You're right, Gunnie," I said, trying to calm him down.

I watched as the tears spilled down his cheeks as he fumbled for his handkerchief and blubbered into it. His eyes barely open.

"But it wasn't, Tobias. You just up and left and took all your bloody horses with you, except you left the biggest one because it was the strongest...but...that..."

A long, sorrowful wail filled the air.

"That was the one that kicked mammy. I had to bury her...why? Why, Tobias, why?"

"I am so very sorry, Gunnie. Really, I am. Will you forgive me?"

"Just get me home., Tobias. Take me home. Back to where we grew up before the bloody nastiness covered the world like some unwanted parasite."

"Okay, Gunnie. Did you want to stay at home?"

"No, dickhead. I want to see it for one last time, you can take me back after I die."

"Righto. You right to get back in?"

"Yeah, on one."

"One," we said in unison.

I made sure he was comfortable and still breathing, secured my drawing stuff and kick-started my Harley. She didn't fire on the first go. I swore under my breath.

"Shush, mammy doesn't like cussing, but flaming heck, Tobias. We gotta go."

"We are!" I replied loudly and put a massive amount of effort into the kick-start.

This time the beautiful note filled the air. I did up my helmet, adjusted the balaclava and twisted the throttle. One solid, dark grey cloud filled the valley ahead of us. According to Bluey's mud-map, in that valley was a disused track which led us to the remains of Gunnie's homestead.

I could tell by the different grasses where the old two-lane road used to be. Praying we wouldn't get a flat tyre; I slowed the bike right down and called out.

"We're nearly there, Gunnie. Where to first?"

"Just keep going until you see the outhouse."

"You need to have a leak?"

"No, you silly old bastard. I want to get something from the cellar, but you have to park near the shed. Do you remember what we put in there?"

"Nope."

He giggled like a young boy. "Good. Glad I've still got my marbles."

I shook my head in bewilderment and wondered what the hell I'd gotten myself into. It seemed my parents' ashes had taken a back seat. We rode for another twenty minutes and managed to dodge the drizzling rain. Surprisingly, the shed was still standing albeit at an awful lean, but it was structural. I parked the bike, helped Gunnie out and escorted him towards what looked like an outhouse.

"How many steps was that?" he suddenly asked.

"Fifteen."

"What? That's seven too many."

I looked at him and his eyes were still shut.

He spoke quickly. "I can see you, Tobias, we've gone too far. Come on, we're running out of light."

I turned him around and we stopped after seven paces. It was as if he was a young man again and easily bent over and felt around in the long grass.

"Well, I'll be," he said quietly and stood up holding a tattered end of an old hemp rope. Following it downwards, he pulled, grunted and pulled again. I bent down beside him, put my hand lower down and pulled as he did.

"Yes!" he exclaimed happily.

"Step back, Gunnie, that's a lot of stale air down there, mate."

"Yeah, yeah, don't light up, Tobias, we'll meet the Maker before we're ready. You got a torch?"

"Back in a moment."

"Now Tobias! Remember, it'll be night soon and we've got to get down there and out of here. We'll go back to your place for the night."

"It's been a while, Gunnie, you remember how to get there?"

"Wise-arse, I practically lived at your place. Your ma was a better cook, mine was better at sewing."

That was a nice piece of information, I mused and shone the torch-light into the depths of darkness, only to be presented with a circle of illuminated dust.

"Off you go, Tobias, I'm no good with stairs anymore, even ones cut out into the dirt wall."

"What am I looking for when I get there?"

"Really? You forgotten that too? The old army trunk. Hurry up!"

I found a pebble and tossed it into the dark abyss and counted to five. It wasn't a very deep hole in the ground and felt around for cut-outs in the side wall for steps. How in the hell did these men do this? The hemp rope was, thankfully, still strong, as I supported my height and weight downwards.

"It'll be eleven paces...and..."

"Ouch!" I bellowed.

"Mind your head then it slopes downwards after six. Pace out another eleven to your right."

I was so tempted to call him a rude name and wondered what my dad would have said while I followed the pathway. I couldn't resist and shone the light over the dirt wall and grinned. Sandstone, into clay and right near the bottom was quartz and ironstone then gravel. It smelt of gold, but awfully deep. I hoped I could take this secret to the grave with me. But not any time soon. I cursed when I hit my head again at the same time, I kicked a metal trunk.

"Frigging hell, Gunnie, what the hell's in here?"

"You really don't remember? Come on, man. You were the one that got it all out, I just had to help you hide it."

"Did we steal it?" I asked in surprise.

"No, you bloody idiot! Our pa's blasted and dug it. You really don't remember?"

"No. And where are we're going to put this thing?"

"By my feet, dickhead. Only need the contents, we leave the trunk."

Even though I was astonished with the revelation and his constant use of my dad's name, my tolerance was running low with all the rude names I was being called. Not too many men dared swear at me, even though I had worked with some rough blokes on some pretty baron, aggressive fields where tempers ran very high. I imagined the bulging eye and suppressed a chuckle. There was no saying the old boy could suddenly forget what he was doing and drop the lid. I grunted as I dragged the trunk, backtracking my steps with a lowered head.

"You done?" he growled.

I swung around and felt air swish past my face. It was then I realised he was sitting on the edge of the hole, swinging his legs.

"Far out, Gunnie! You scared the crap out of me and nearly kicked me in the head."

"Tobias Otto Gutterman, get a bloody move on. We have to get the hell out of here and you need to cover the tracks for the last time in your life. Here's the key. Hand me the bags."

Something hit my chest and plopped onto the dirt. Shining the torch downwards, I saw a heavy old key and promptly cleaned it off before inserting it into the lock. It took some muscle, but eventually I got it opened and bit my lip until it bled. Nine draw-string cloth bags sat neatly in the bottom. I needed two hands to lift most of them out, except one. Gunnie took them like they were all filled with air.

"That's nine, that's all of them. Come on, Tobias, close it up and toss the lock and key into the darkness. We've got to go now."

I did as he instructed.

"We're good to go, Gunnie."

He held out his hand which I clasped firmly. "We'll shake again when we're back at your place. Hurry up."

He dropped the lid, pulled out a knife and wound up the loose rope. I just stared and kept quiet.

We had travelled fifteen miles when Gunnie slapped me on the leg and held up his hand. I slowed to a stop.

"Mate," he yelled above the rumbling idle, "My right hand tells you which direction, my left tells you how many miles."

"Got it," I yelled back, not commenting that we'd been doing it that way all day.

Just as darkness fell, we turned down a lane and travelled for two more miles. I had never ridden my bike at night time and was surprised, and relieved, at the brightness of the headlight. Gunnie slapped me on the leg forcing me to slow down quickly. I shone the torchlight downwards just enough to see his face but not blinding the old boy.

"Three hundred yards to your right is the shortcut we made. Another mile down there and it takes us right to your back door!" He grinned up at me.

My anticipation and excitement were unfathomable and I felt like a little kid about to uncover a huge secret. The last mile seemed to take forever, and boy, the track was rough. Poor Gunnie was going to be covered in bruises by the time he got upright and my butt would take a week to feel normal. My poor bike! As I thought that, an owl swooped in front of us and I hit the brakes sliding in the gravelly dirt.

“Hold on to it, Tobias, ride it out, man. Just like the Billy carts! Woohoo!” Gunnie had gone back to his childhood and was laughing wildly.

I couldn’t help but smile at the sound and joined in. Then my laughter slowly faded away. One last curve and my headlight swept over a wrought-iron railing. It was exactly the same design mum and I had at our home. I pulled up alongside the back landing, helped Gunnie out and escorted him up the stairs.

“Tobias, I came back as often as I could to make it liveable in case. But it’s been a while. There’s a kero lamp and matches just inside the door. I have to catch my breath.”

“In case of what?” I asked as I helped him sit.

“We needed a hideout. Geez, your brain really is scrambled,” he grumbled.

I listened to his ragged breathing and then his incoherent muttering began. I handed him the leather drinking pouch and held it up to his lips.

“Gunnie, you need a drink. It’s been a hell of a run! Steady, not too much.”

I left him with the water and managed to open the door. I’m guessing he hadn’t been back for at least five years given the accumulation of dust, dirt and water damage, but it was surprisingly rodent free. Then I saw why. The biggest snake skin hung from the rafters. Stepping out quietly, I lit the lamp and hung it on the post.

“Tobias, can you bring the bag that’s right on top please. We’ll live on that for the night and work out a plan tomorrow. You right with that?”

"Sure, Gunnie. I'll take the first watch, you sleep for six hours, then we swap."

"Yeah, that's good, Tobias."

He shuffled over to the post and rested his head against it and very soon was snoring. I retrieved the bag he asked for, my saddlebags and the swag. I swore the man could see through closed eyes.

"Goodo, let's eat. Beans and bully-beef and probably some damned hard biscuits, but we're back in those days where we don't care, hey, Tobias?"

"That's it, Gunnie. Hey, I've got a tube of condensed milk if you want a sugar hit."

"Typical Tobias, always thinking of the sweet things in life."

I didn't comment and rolled out the swag for the old boy but I desperately wanted to know the story behind the other eight bags!

"Hey Tobias, you never did say why you came back," he said quietly.

"I'm fulfilling a request and returning two people home."

"Yeah? How?"

"Their ashes are in urns."

"Oh. You gonna bury them?"

"No. I'm going to scatter them. I believe that's what they wanted. A home would be better than in an abandoned field, I reckon."

"Yeah, too many already there. Do they both come from here?"

"No."

"Were they in love?"

"Yeah, I reckon they were."

His light snoring got louder so I gently eased him onto the swag and used my jacket for his pillow. I was going exploring. Taking my torch, I snuck back inside and wondered through the empty shell of a home. The cast iron bed frames were still in place, chipped porcelain and broken crockery laid on the deteriorating shelves. I constantly reminded myself that this was actually my grandparents' house. My father and his mate, Gunnie, called it home. When I found myself back in the room with the snake skin, I was drawn to a narrow passageway parallel to the outside of the house. It led to a door which opened easily. It was obvious someone had frequented it given it was relatively tidy. Two photographs sat on the little bookshelf above the single cast-iron bed frame. I couldn't resist and shone the torchlight over them.

"Yep, that's us!" Gunnie said quietly from behind me.

"Bloody hell, man! You trying to scare the living daylights out of me?" I stepped away swiftly.

He pushed his way through the doorway dragging the swag, "Not tonight. Anyways, you're on lookout remember, this is where I always sleep."

"Righto, night Gunnie."

I didn't know if I wanted to know all their stories now. I felt like an intruder and awfully guilty. By some greater power, I brought my parents back to the home where my father grew up in, along with his best mate, who both got into a lot of mischief and obviously shared a massive secret. I sat on the porch and watched the night sky until I couldn't keep my eyes open. As I drifted off, I heard a soft flurry of wings and dreamt of owls.

Gunnie's wails dragged me out of my dream state, but I was under the eyes of a barn owl when I opened my own. I slowly lifted myself up onto my elbows and stared back into the tawny orbs until it swivelled its head 180 degrees and didn't move. The wailing got louder and soon I was in my dad's old room. The old boy had ended up underneath the bed frame, his sleeve had gotten hooked up on the rusty springs.

"It's okay, Gunnie, I'll get you out. Don't move." I spoke quietly and firmly.

"Please hurry, Tobias, I have to take watch." He sounded desperate.

"Not for a few hours yet. Everything's quiet. We're safe."

He seemed to settle down as I supported his arm and unwound the barb from the button hole near the wrist.

"I'm sorry I was angry with you," he murmured.

"I'm sorry about your pappy, mammy and grandpappy," I replied softly.

"I hated you for stealing my girl, then leaving me to deal with all the death, but man, you were an ace on the horses. I remember watching you jump on them like that bloody movie star, but I'll always remember the way you scooped me up out of the road of the runaway wagon. It was loaded, remember? Yeah, it was loaded with all the mail and bonds and such. We found the drivers clinging to the trees overhanging the ravine. You...you made me wait beside that big ol' gum..."

I finally managed to get him untangled and supported his arm while he rubbed his wrist.

"You remember how scared they were? No, you wouldn't because you're losing your marbles. Do you want to hear the story, Tobias?"

"Yes, Gunnie I do."

"Okay, well, you told them to tie the rope around their waists and shimmy down the bark until they were over the edge. They were terrified, but your voice was strong. I was terrified and couldn't look at you in case your bad eye bulged. Anyways, you promised them if they kept a hold of the rope, you'd pull them back over the ledge. Tobias, how you got those bloody horses to walk backwards I will never know, but man, you did and those two drivers survived."

He opened his eyes and stared at me blankly. "YOU saved them, Tobias."

It was an accusation. I think I was beginning to work out where his and my father's relationship had broken down and desperately needed fixing before it was far too late.

"WE did, Gunnie. You were there too. Don't reckon I could have done it without you."

"Me? What'd I do?"

"You were always there for me and I let you down," I said sadly.

"Aw, gee man, it was a long time ago. But we're rich, Tobias. You and your bloody horse, skimming up and down that ravine retrieving the mail and such. The cops were relieved. Did you know it was their pay in the metal trunk you pulled up for them?"

"No! Had no idea."

"Well, they didn't care about the other trunk. Don't think they ever knew about it really. Our pa's were taking shortcuts but you and those bloody horses." He coughed, then muttered, "Now we're rich and we're too bloody old to do what we were going to do!"

"I can't remember what we were going to do!"

He rolled his eyes. "Geez, Tobias, you're hard work these days. We were going to take the Steamer up to Queensland and party with those meter maids! Gold for the gold." He sighed heavily. "Well, that's what we sung for a while anyway."

Gunnie fell silent then and turned away from me. I genuinely felt sad.

"I'm sorry, Gunnie."

His frail old body wracked with his sobbing. "Yeah, so am I. If only the bloody world had let us play our games, we would have been so happy for so much longer."

"Yeah, that's for sure."

"Go and see if there are any eggs in the chook pen, Tobias, you're up for breakfast."

"Sure, Gunnie. Catch you later."

# Chapter Five

Under the kero lamplight, I wondered aimlessly and carefully through the long grass around the old house. I had no idea what I was looking for, I didn't know the house or the size of the land or anything about it. I couldn't even make a telephone call to Bluey and ask. There hadn't been any civilisation in these parts for decades. At times I was confused. Gunnie was definitely confused, shellshocked, but with a wealth of tales keeping my father alive. Yet, I felt like an impostor but didn't have the heart to break the old boy's spirit, or heart. But I did reckon he needed to be back with Bluey and his buddies at the pub.

I sat down on the front porch and smiled sadly at the wrought iron railing. Yeah, if only the world had let them play their games. I turned down the lamp and listened to the dawn chorus bringing on the new day. The deep red splash across the horizon was a definite indicator the day would end up with a storm. By the time the sun made its presence known, I had located the abandoned chook pen, the dilapidated shed protecting a very rusty Chamberlain tractor and what looked like an avenue of trees. They definitely weren't fruit trees. Some had survived and had tiny yellow buds on them. As I got closer, I realised they were Wattles. I strolled through the middle of the two rows and counted thirty a side. I knew that generally an avenue of trees led to some sort of architectural or landscape feature. Nothing at the far end. I turned around, peering in vain through the early sunrays as to what I would discover.

By the time I counted to forty-two, it was a bit of both. A weed-covered wishing well. I tore away at the strangling growth until it was standing in all its glory. Its roof was still intact. I dropped in a pebble, listened intently and counted silently. Fifty-five and a faint splash! That's one very deep well. I stepped back and admired the cobblestone structure and wondered why the house hadn't been built of the same stone. That's when I looked at the soil. It wasn't fertile. There was no way any crop would grow on that land, even sheep would battle to survive. These rocks didn't come from here! What did my grandparents do for an income? How did they survive? Gold?

I found Gunnie boiling the billy over an open fire underneath my dad's bedroom window. He appeared to be in good spirits and looked younger, if that were even possible.

"Morning Tobias, any eggs?"

"Morning Gunnie, not today."

"Never mind."

"Did you know how deep that well went?"

His eyes filled with tears.

"Bloody hell, idiot. Your old man loved dynamite..."

"Oh man, I'm sorry."

We didn't speak for a while, but he sure knew how to boil a good brew. I told him so and received a grunt in reply.

Eventually he rinsed out his mug and looked away. "These people you're taking home, do you know where?"

"This place is as good as any. It's a home with some good memories in it. . .do you think the folk would mind?"

"Do you remember anything?" he asked incredulously.

"No, Gunnie. It's bloody annoying, I know, but help me out here, would you? Please?"

He let out a massive sigh, shifted in the old canvas sling chair and talked like it was yesterday.

"Me mammy always talked about the daring ventures of your pa. Gold hunting, blowing things up to see what was under it, planting native trees to encourage wildlife and to use the petal dust for paint. Those Wattle trees, geez our hands were busted up and bled after planting them during the school holidays. Your ma had the patience of a saint and would go along with just about everything he did. Those were my mammy's words, mind. You and me had to go and help cart the stones for the wishing well, Tobias. We was just kids, but the women didn't want us pinching the tarts so we learnt how to mix mortar while our pa's protected the hole your dad blew."

Gunnie burst out laughing then.

"Your ma was so mad. You and I crept under their window and listened to them arguing then they suddenly stopped. We looked up and they tipped a bucket of water onto us as punishment for eavesdropping. That was our first lesson in architecture, your pa said!"

I had to laugh.

"Anyways, that's how the wishing well came about. God knows how many pennies are down there, but it's a long ways down and I'm not caring to get them out. And don't you bloody well think about it either, Tobias. You'd forget your way and get lost down there!"

"I've been down enough holes lately thanks, Gunnie!"

“Oh yeah, you forgot about that too. We have to shake.”

He struggled to get out of the chair and accepted my assistance. He threw his shoulders back and thrust out his right hand. I followed suit and was genuinely surprised at the strength of his handshake.

“Tobias Otto Gutterman, to us, our friendship and even split of the proceeds. Let’s shake.”

“To us, Gunnie, our friendship and even split of the proceeds. Let’s shake.”

“You’ve forgotten my name, haven’ t you?” he challenged.

I had to think very quickly.

“Have I ever called you anything else but Gunnie?”

He looked at me strangely, frowned, scratched his ear and burst out laughing. “No, I don’t think you have. Okay, let’s shake again.”

We did and got lost in our own thoughts. I was suddenly grateful of my bristly three-day growth to hide the dimples. Nothing I could do about the dark hair, but the dimples may have been my undoing. I still felt like an impostor though, but I prayed this helped Gunnie.

“Don’t suppose you remember the old folk scratching their initials on the cobblestones, do you?”

“You’re right, Gunnie. I don’t.”

With childlike excitement, he asked, “Wanna go and see if we can find them?”

“You bet!”

I walked alongside Gunnie as he confidently strolled in the direction of the wishing well. I was amazed and quite confronted at the same time with how the mind and memory worked. We peered at all the stones, with each one stained in green from the weedy vines or presumably mould. I just had to know more.

"Why do you think they carved their initials into the stones?" I asked cautiously.

"Der, because they were in love."

"Of course."

Right at the moment, I knew where I would be scattering my parent's ashes.

"Gunnie, you probably told me this, but your folk...they're buried up north..."

"So are yours, you dickhead..."

"Yeah, okay, but why there?"

"Flaming heck, you really are cooked in the brain. Our little town never had a graveyard so the big town, the damn rich town took all our dead. All our dead. Nearly our whole town went away to war and those that didn't tried in vain to survive. The big town took everyone away from here in one way or the other. I returned to the joint after every tour. Had nowhere else to go but I could go to where they lay."

"Should we leave them there?"

"Well, there's stuff all left of our fathers and I ain't about to dig up my mammy. So yes. We leave them there."

I was treading dangerous waters now.

"If I died, would you scatter me here, Gunnie?"

"It's the only place for you. For me too. The house I grew up in got burnt to the ground in a bushfire. There's nothing left except what you saw, so yeah, scatter me here will you!"

"I prayed to my folk last night and asked if they wouldn't mind if I scattered two people's ashes around their home."

Gunnie snickered, "What reply did you get?"

"Dunno, but I saw an owl."

He burst out laughing and turned towards the house. "Well, it's not as if they're going to clip you around the ears. I'll go and clean up and get ready to head back north while you do what you've got to do."

Breaking apart the urns was possibly the hardest thing I have ever had to do in my life. Not only emotionally, but man, why do they make the containers so awkwardly difficult to get open? It was just as well I had a flat-head screwdriver in the bottom of my saddlebag. Gunnie watched from afar with a quizzical look on his face but didn't say anything as I held a container aloft in each hand. I prayed and wept and prayed again, begged the Good Lord to forgive me and to bless my parents in their eternal life as I watched their ashes freely converge around the wishing well and let the breeze take them where it felt they ought to be. I stood there numbly watching the dust disperse and settle until a distant rumbling broke my reverie. Gunnie's loud, gruff voice spurred me into action.

"Hey, Tobias? Sorry man, but we've got to go before Mother Nature has her way with us."

I listened to each container plop into the underground pool and wiped the last of my tears on my shirt, as I whispered my farewell.

"You will always be in my heart, mum and dad. Thank you for your love. Until we meet again."

Gunnie was already in the sidecar and spoke sternly as I approached.

"Your four bags are in the saddlebags, mine are by my feet. Before we go, we have to tell each other our final wishes. What do you want?"

"Man, do we have to do this now?" I didn't mean to, but I whined.

"Yes, we do. I'll go first, you chicken-livered, yellow belly. Two bags go to Bluey and the rest get split up between the old boys at the pub. My ashes get spread around this wishing well too. Your turn."

"The same, I suppose."

"Bulldust, Tobias Otto Gutterman. You got a family to take care of. If you want to give Bluey something, just give him one bag. He'll never spend what its worth in his lifetime anyway."

"Okay, Bluey has one bag, I'll take the other three and my ashes get spread around this wishing well too."

"An oath?"

"An oath, Gunnie."

"Good. We've got to go now, Tobias."

We made it back to the pub just as the heaven's opened up and pushed the bike through the interior, through the back door and down the keg ramp until it was safely tucked away in the shed. Several rounds were on the house as was a very welcome and hearty dinner. I bade my cohorts a goodnight and stumbled up the stairs.

It was nearing midnight when a quiet knock disturbed my concentration. I opened the door to find Bluey standing there holding two beers.

"A nightcap?" I asked with a grin and stepped aside so he could enter the room.

"Yeah, mate. Don't know how else to thank you. Here's cheers!"

"Cheers! It is I that needs to thank you."

We drank our beers in companionable silence. I couldn't hold back.

"Bluey, you have to let me know when Gunnie passes away. I swore an oath."

"Yeah, he's just cornered me on my way up and said the same." He looked at me intently and asked quietly, "How'd you pull it off?"

"I felt guilty the whole time, man, I still do but I figured it didn't make sense to prevent someone from reliving their childhood. And we cleared the air. I discovered a lot of things about my folk and myself. But I realised how deep the hurt was and smoothed the painful edges, I hope."

"He sure looked..."

"Relieved?"

"Yeah, relieved. Good word for it. So, what are you going to do now, Toby?"

"If you don't mind, I'll camp up here for a while. I've got some paperwork to do and then head off. Um...is there a picture framer in town?"

"A what?"

I repeated myself and held up the sketch of Gunnie.

"Good God, that's a masterpiece! Far out, man, you captured him perfectly. Ah yeah, on the corner of Second and Fifth, they're in with the florist believe it or not."

"Thanks for the compliment, but I just dabble."

"You have to give that to him before you go."

"What if it undoes everything he's experienced recently and accuses me of being a traitor or cruel?"

"That'll only be a short-term thing, son. He won't remember those words, I swear. Now you make sure you put your name on that piece. That's a one-off."

"Well, it's Gunnie's and then it's up to you who the caretaker is after that."

"An oath?"

"An oath, Bluey."

He smiled, nodded his head as we shook hands and murmured our farewells as he closed the door behind him.

Three weeks later, my bike was back to its original condition, albeit with a few stone chips describing its eventful journey, and it was my last night. The framed picture of Gunnie was wrapped in blue satin and strategically positioned on the top shelf along with the spirits. The pub was at its limits with the patrons and several special guests had journeyed a fair distance to be at the presentation for Gunnie. The barmaid had made some phone calls and discovered that the old boy was one of five who were still alive from his original Battalion. She had encouraged them all to have a private get-together in the shed with Bluey being the emcee, before bringing them back into the pub. The rest of us all pitched in and rearranged the tables so it looked quite formal with Gunnie's seat at the head of the table and his mates flanking him. I was as nervous as all hell and really didn't want to stay for dinner, but, like it is with Mrs Smallwood, when the barmaid put down her knitting, I paid attention.

There were lots of conversations, loud laughter, some tears and the five older men had the floor at any given time. They were celebrated, honoured and thanked for their Service to their country. Their fallen mates were remembered for their ultimate sacrifice with a minute's silence. Bluey then stood up and tapped a spoon against his glass. Silence again befell the pub. He looked at me and encouraged me to stand.

"Gentlemen, we have in our presence another man with a lot of history and a lot of living to do. I'll hand it over to you now, sonny."

"Thank you, Bluey. Gentlemen, I take my hat off to you all. You're a fine set of examples and I have a dedication to Gunnie."

"Ahh, sit down, Esquire," he grumbled.

I'd caught him staring at me regularly during dinner, either smirking, frowning or nodding his head. I prayed his internal conversation was a kind one and grinned at him.

"I will, Sir, but I want you to have this first." I walked behind the bar, easily reached the satin-wrapped parcel and went and stood beside Gunnie.

I had to clear my throat several times to eventually be able to speak clearly.

"Words cannot describe my eternal gratitude to you. I too, am a man of my oath and handshake, Gunnie. Thank you for who are you, your tales of youth and for showing me who I am."

I held my out hand which he shook heartily and looked me square in the eyes.

"Bloody Gutterman with their horses and their shovels," he smirked and winked.

Bluey and I assisted him to stand up and stood by as he revealed the charcoal sketch. We caught him as he stumbled backwards and eased him back into his chair.

"How?" He stared at me, back at the framed picture, back at me.

"When you rode shotgun, Sir."

His raucous laughter was contagious and beckoned me closer to his face.

In a hushed, hoarse voice, he said, "Thank you, I'll treasure it. You're a good man. Our words are our bond as are our handshakes. Thank you for letting me be me, Junior. Your ma and pa would be proud of you. Go and have a good life and remember the three bags full, and so shall your life be."

I gently squeezed his shoulder as a large tear plopped onto his chest pocket. He smudged it into the fabric and wiped away one of his own. We saluted each other, nodded formally then grinned.

# Chapter Six

On the sixteenth of November in the baking heat of the Yunta outback, I had just documented my geological report and was contemplating my future when I received a telegram from Bluey.

"Sad news STOP Gunnie's out of ammo STOP Ready to ride shotgun STOP"

I sat under the shade of a Gidgee tree and wept. After sending my reply to Bluey, I sent a telegram to Mrs Smallwood explaining another family matter would delay my return and her niece was welcome to stay into the New Year.

With a little over 120 kilograms of gold evenly distributed in my saddle bags, I rolled through the town three days later with my helmet off and walked my bike to the front of the Fallen Soldier Memorial. From my saddlebag I retrieved the wreath of poppies and found a place for my tribute to Gunnie. I said several prayers, took a deep breath and wondered if Bluey had discovered the single bag stashed in the footwell of the sidecar.

The pub patrons were understandably solemn, yet the late afternoon sun brought another piece of artwork to life as Gunnie sat proudly underneath the copper magnificence. Even with his gruff disposition, the memory of his inner child hanging onto a Billy cart would always make me smile.

~Rest In Peace all ye,
For who you were,
For what you did,
An indebted memory~

**The End**

# GOLD, DUST, and DIRTY SECRETS

Lorie Brink

# Gold, Dust, and Dirty Secrets

Lorie Brink

Lorie Brink

B&W image by Lorie Brink

# Contents

# Comfort Zone

With lives turned upside down and now victims of circumstance, there was no way they could ever return to Cooktown.

Their elbows bug-smashed from keeping the doors of the old Vauxhall ute from flying open, Nelson and Clara longed to crest the rugged hill. Crumbling remains of Maytown and the isolated historic Goldfields calmed the frayed nerves of the teenagers.

Their hasty escape in the darkest hour, fraught with incomprehensible danger.

# A Good Reason To Run!

The young'uns and good friends for most of their lives—he of Chinese descent, she a half-caste Aboriginal—had been in the wrong place at the wrong time upon the shores of Archer's Point. Their entwinement on the beach rudely interrupted when distant torchlight swept over their half-naked bodies.

Discarded shirts left crumpled on the sand as they fled for the shadows of the rockface. Using the darkened patches and trunks of the massive palm trees that lined the beach as decoys, they escaped into their secret cave created amongst the rocky dunes. Pressing themselves against the cold walls, dared to breathe as two angry male voices got louder.

'Hey Finn, did ya see where they went?'

'Nah, just a pair of kids playin' nooky on the beach. They wouldn't have seen anythin'. Come on, Shorty, let's go, we gotta get these fish unloaded and use the tide.'

'Fish? They're bloody dugongs, ya idiot. Told ya we should never have got caught up in this. Only the Abos are allowed to catch and eat these. But no, ya always been a greedy bastard.'

'Oi, best you shut your trap eh! You're no clean skin, mate. You been shiftin' drugs when you're not fishin'. Your kid ain't no fool neither, he's been askin' questions. After all, it is the happy hippy era.'

'He's my stepson and a throwback. Leave him out of this, Finn.'

'From what I hear your grandkids are going to be half black, half Chinese. Isn't this his shirt, mate?'

'At least he's Aussie, mate.'

'Watch it.'

'That shirt better bloody not be his. He'll be nothin' to me if it is and she'll have a tough time stayin' in this one-horse town. I'll see to that. Come on, let's get outta here. We gotta catch that tide.'

After a while, the pair of teenagers crept out of their hiding place. They didn't speak, just held each other's hand tightly as the young man led the way.

Like a death knell, two aluminium dinghies clanged in the incoming tide. Heavy thuds punched the calm night air. Muffled voices and supressed laughter drifted along the shoreline. Nelson and Clara shimmied along the rocky dune and prayed they wouldn't be spotted as they made their way to the path that led upwards to the lookout and carpark.

Too late! A sweeping floodlight from the boats sprung them like kangaroos in a headlight. Fortunately for them, they were more familiar with the outcrop and quickest path to the carpark than their would-be captors. Ducking, weaving and dodging ricocheting bullets, they managed to scramble unscathed to the lad's rough-and-ready Ute.

Slamming through the gears, they screamed when a bullet smashed the passenger side-mirror. Neither spoke a word. They hardly breathed. They had to grab enough belongings and get the heck out of town. They knew who the men were.

# For The Love of Gold, and Old Mrs D

Often foregoing food for fuel, camping rough and bathing in creeks, Nelson and Clara now had to get used to looking over their shoulder. Their journey took them along the Peninsula Development Road, where giant rugged outcrops loomed ominously and the familiar loneliness of the dirt track in the dark night made everything more eerie.

The young'uns loved the adventure of getting to Maytown with its bulldust, rough tracks and spooky mountainous surroundings, but as the Painter's brush dabbed soft hues of pink on the cloudy dawn, they had to find somewhere to hide for the day. Being sure someone would be sent to look for them they cautiously turned off the rutted track towards an ancient riverbed. Navigating over the dry rubbly path until the bend in the old river, the towering Burdekin plums a refreshing sight. Another favourite place of theirs to camp and fossick, and where the ute would be out of sight.

They hankered to get to their preferred destination of the haunted Goldfields. This glorious mineral had given them hope when they first stumbled across a forgotten tailings mound. Painstakingly panning and manually combing through the dirt pile, they found enough gold flecks and tiny nuggets earning them much more than their combined meagre monthly wage.

Nelson and Clara had become friendly with a bushie who always seemed to have cash and happily traded the gold for a fair price. He also paid for extra supplies of flour, salt and jerky. Their first meeting was just outside the consecrated Chinese Cemetery when the young'uns were changing a flat tyre. The man emerged silently from the scrub. His metal detector, pick and young Blue Heeler dog were as threatening as his stature. Clara had instantly locked herself in the cab, while Nelson defended her virtue, and did his best to conceal his fear.

After a wary conversation, the dog seemed to be very relaxed around the young'uns and happily accepted their pats. From thereon, the man seemed to *come across them* and shared tales of the Palmer River Goldfields. They never tired of his history lessons. His quiet, emotional voice taking them on incredible mind journeys. But their favourite was the 1870s goldrush and alluvial mining being the drawcard for the Chinese. The Orientals arrived in Cooktown by the shiploads, and walked single file for endless miles carrying their wares hung on bamboo sticks slung across their shoulders. It was a one-way journey for some, and an extremely prosperous journey for others with tonnes of gold illegally shipped back to China in their death-urns. Hostility between the Australians, Aboriginals and Chinese was also rife.

There were several powerful yet competitive Chinese families controlling the mineral fields and business houses in Cooktown during its heyday, with the rivalry continuing down through the generations. When the young'uns had asked the man how he knew about this, he explained that he was he was the grandnephew of the headman on the docks of Cooktown. Furthermore, he was the only son of a second-generation

Australian-Chinese woman that had worked in an Opium Den. Mixed blood always brought about mixed feelings.

The bushie had endured very cruel years growing up, and at the tender age of 14, stowed away on the first Railmotor that ran on the Cooktown-Laura Line. He'd trekked south along the old Cobb & Co coach road, keeping his head down until he met an old Aboriginal. The Elder taught him how to track, hunt, prospect and survive. That was nearly 40 years ago and this bushie owed that old Aboriginal man his life. Both men had avoided conscription and numerous devastating cyclones. Cooktown became a victim of its isolation too.

Over the decades, the bushie had seen his mother several times from afar as the town slowly died. It was only when she was on her deathbed that he sat with her and told her his story. She passed away holding his hand, at peace instead of broken-hearted. He always stopped his reminisce there. The young'uns knew there was more to his story and desperately wanted to know more. Yet, too shy to ask, they respected the bushie's silence.

***

During the last three years, Nelson and Clara had learnt more about survival, common sense and practical skills from the man in the bush, than they had been taught at school. They sensibly used the traded cash to do night classes with Old Mrs D whenever they could. Nelson wanted to have his own mechanic business and Clara wanted to become a veterinarian. Old Mrs D wasn't really a tutor. She was a widow who had watched the youngsters mature, taught them how to work to a budget, given them access to encyclopedias and initiated correspondence courses without any hesitation. Inexplicably, they had all found solace in each other's company.

As minors, Nelson and Clara's homelife had been awfully cruel, and when Old Mrs D caught them pinching fruit from her garden, she had taken pity on them instantly. As a long-term outsider, Old Mrs D kept aloof of the townsfolk, knew what went on, who were good people and who weren't. This particular pair of misfits hadn't been the only kids she had secretly nurtured and helped escape the town's clutches to hopefully make a decent life of their own.

More recently, Nelson had put into practice the hands-on mechanical knowledge gained from their bushie friend and rebuilt Old Mrs D's Willys Jeep in her carport, while Clara learnt how to mend and cook hearty meals with minimal ingredients.

# Expressions

At long last, they felt safe. Laying on their stomachs watching the dancing flames of their simple fire licking the stew pot, silent tears fell with relief and sorrow. Clara rested her head on her folded arms, sniffling quietly.

Nelson reached over and stroked her head. 'I have no words to comfort you but I'm sure you share my anguish in not saying goodbye to Old Mrs D.'

'You're right. We have to get word to her somehow. She'll be frantic,' Clara whispered.

Lost in their own thoughts, neither moved until a twig snapped like a gunshot. In a flash Clara dived into the ute, pulled the heavy door shut as quietly as possible, and crammed herself against the firewall. Nelson wriggled backwards and propped himself against the front tyre. His left hand clutched the nulla-nulla. He didn't even think about extinguishing the fire. He gasped as something wet touched his hand and nearly wet himself with relief when he recognised the Blue Heeler.

'Hey pooch, where's your master?'

A familiar voice floated through the mild night air. 'Over here, didn't want to startle you too much. Best get Clara some fresh air, eh.'

As Nelson tapped on the window, Clara's scared face popped up. Seeing his smile, she unlocked the door.

'It's okay, come out now, we have visitors,' he encouraged warmly.

Taking Nelson's hand, Clara smiled at the bushie, 'Hello, Mister.'

Dipping his hat, 'Evening Clara.'

He felt the warmth coming off the bonnet and frowned. 'What's going on?'

Nelson approached the man and indicated they should sit by the fire. 'Clara, please bring another plate for our friend. The stew is almost ready. We know pooch would have been fed.'

The Blue Heeler stood patiently beside Clara as she knelt down and patted him. She had recently learnt that dogs' hips could be a weakness and put to practice how to test their flexibility. Gently, she stretched his hind legs backwards while talking softly to him.

Nelson sighed and sat down heavily on the ground, 'Sir, we witnessed something illegal on the beach and had to leave quickly. We were recognised, shot at, and fled with only a few things. It's too dangerous for us to go back.'

'This should be good! What did you see?'

'It's more about what we heard. Illegal meat traders but with dugongs. The two men are known to us but . . . not sure who shot at us.'

'The men? Who are they?'

Taking out his embarrassment and anger on the soup pot, Nelson replied, 'My stepfather and his best mate. Shonky bastards.'

'Enough of the language when there are women around. You and I shall go for a walk before dawn, then we speak like men.'

'Yes, Sir. Thank you.'

Clara ignored the latter conversation as she handed out the three bowls and spoons.

During dinner, Nelson elaborated on the previous night's adventure, where they hid during the day until arriving at Maytown long after dark. They had to be sure they weren't being followed. Not even Old Mrs D had ever asked where they got to, although they thought she had her suspicions.

'Hmm. Tell me more about this Old Mrs D,' the bushie stated curiously.

Clara jumped at the opportunity and described the history, their friendship and the kindness the dear lady had showed them. They had only ever known her as Old Mrs D. After she married a Polish man, nobody could pronounce her surname, so the 'D' stuck. In the early days of her marriage, she was referred to as Mrs D but widowed a few years in and as time passed, she inherited the 'Old' bit. Clara enthusiastically described the correspondence courses they were both studying and how Nelson was applying his mechanical knowledge with an old Willys Jeep.

Clara wiped her eyes, 'It's just so sad that we had to leave without telling her, Mister. She will be very worried; of that I know. Any suggestions how we can get word to her?'

The man toyed with his long wispy beard. 'I need to go and visit an old friend soon, perhaps I can drop a note in her letterbox.'

'That'd be terrific! Thanks Mister,' Clara excitedly replied.

'Don't get your hopes up,' he said gently, 'I can't afford to get mixed up in any trouble, but tell me, who's the head coppa nowadays?'

Nelson scoffed in disdain. 'His nickname is Plod, but goes by Brutus Trent and he's a blow-in. The gossip around town is that his real name got changed because he did something wrong down south and got shifted out of the way.'

'You keep your ear to the ground, I gather?' the man asked gently.

'Have to, Sir, else we'd be skinned alive. We've grown up together, similar horrid homelife, different bloodlines and mixed blood too. Street smart, but determined to make a better life for ourselves. We don't want to be dobbers neither.'

'You reckon this cop would be interested in the trade that goes on?'

'Nah, I've seen him and a few other crooks around town having conversations outside the copshop plus regular drug deals with the latest waitress behind the pub. I'm lucky I haven't been sprung, but they're often too drunk or preoccupied to notice me,' Nelson coughed and paused before continuing.

'See, we've been lucky to keep our jobs at the supermarket. The bulk food storage container is out the back and it's easy to overhear conversations. I've also seen them when a woman's voice can be heard across the carpark to the pub. It's obvious what they're all doing. She's a friendly thing, even more at night. We've written down what we've witnessed in a journal which is kept out at Old Mrs D's place. It's got several years of entries in it. Old Mrs D doesn't know about the journal, but she's been in town probably the longest. That lady is no fool I can tell you, but we would never forgive ourselves if she got caught up in our drama.'

'About the illegal fishing, are you saying it's a regular thing?'

'Yes! Every second month without fail . . . but the other night was unusual. There's a big buyer down south. The dugongs and turtles are brought in on the incoming tide. The men beach the boats, then transfer the catch to a different tinny. As the tide recedes, the two boats are pushed back and tack along the shoreline in different directions. You can tell by the sound of the boat motors that one is carrying a heavier load. There's an old ramp that's accessible during high tide in a nearby estuary. Sir, do you remember as a lad if they shot crocodiles that got too cheeky?'

The man chuckled. 'Only too well. Shooting anything that got too cheeky was a sport in those days!'

Clara smothered a giggle while Nelson laughed freely before stopping suddenly at the man's next question.

'What about your respective mothers? What occupies their time? That is, if you don't mind me asking?'

Clara hung her head and Nelson reached over and squeezed her hand.

In a sad voice he said, 'My mother tries her best but sadly is addicted to alcohol. I think she drinks to drown her guilt or fear. I've begged her to leave but she won't, or can't. I'm not sure which.'

Clara sighed despondently, 'Mister, mine was a very good teacher on one of the missions but had a fling with the town's headmaster. I was only young, my father who also drinks found out. The headmaster disappeared and my mother has been scared since. I've secretly given her money to help with the rent since I was 12, but she's never been a woman to show any affection towards me. I'm an only child and like Nelson and you, of mixed blood.'

A companionable silence fell over the three as they watched the flames. The pooch's ears pricked up as a gentle breeze whispered through the trees.

'Clara, that was a very tasty stew. I suppose Old Mrs D had a lot to do with it?'

The night and her olive skin hid the blush that crept over her cheeks. She wasn't used to compliments and shyly replied, 'Thank you, Mister and yes Old Mrs D had everything to do with it.'

Abruptly the man stood up and instantly his Blue Heeler was standing beside him. 'Listen, young'uns, I'll take my groceries and leave you be. Lay low for a few days, use the cavern if you need to. It's large enough for your jalopy here but make sure you do not venture further than your normal area. There've been new visitors and they're not pleasant. Keep your wits about you more than what you normally do. Okay?'

Nelson was standing and shook the man's hand. 'Yes, we will. Thank you for listening and joining us for dinner, Sir.'

'No worries, son. Clara, thanks again. Night.'

'Good night, Mister and thank you.'

Nelson helped drag the man's groceries off the end of the ute's tray and watched as he carried them one item at a time before disappearing into the shadow of a rocky outcrop. He returned carrying a bundle of firewood and plonked it on the tray.

'Geez, thanks Sir.'

'Nelson, we will have that man's talk but not tomorrow's dawn. Look after yourselves and each other. See you around.'

The young'uns stood there speechless as they watched the bushie and his dog blend into the tree line and silently disappear into the night.

Clara clutched Nelson's hand, 'What happened?'

Shrugging his shoulders, 'Not sure, but we are not to question this man's behaviour. He must have his reasons and we need to respect that. Come on, let's clean up.'

# Can't Help Who You Fall In Love With

By the sixth morning, both young'uns were on tender hooks, and dangerously low on water. Having remembered how the pioneers and livestock perished by drinking the stagnant waters in the creeks they weren't going to take any risks, not even for a bath.

They had shifted camp twice, slowly making their way to the cavern. As that day's shadows got longer, they eventually pushed the heavy Ute backwards as far it would go into the dark, cool void. The bushie had woven leaf and bark together which hung from a branch, disguising the opening perfectly.

Having a dark camp at night was safest with only a little fire during the day for cooking. Motors echoed across the valleys which coincided with spot fires on the opposite ridges every night since their arrival. Their bathing water was nearly depleted and they were extremely conscious and embarrassed about their body odours.

Trying to encourage conversation to take their minds off the long night ahead, Clara asked, 'Nelson, do you think we can ever stop the illegal meat trade?'

'When we're older and not living in a cave, anything's possible!' he laughed softly.

Distant rumbling caught their attention nearing midnight. They feared it was someone blasting dynamite, but the moisture in the air brought mixed relief. Instantly they positioned three buckets in a clearing away from the cavern. No sooner had they stepped back inside, the sky lit up with sheet lightning. It crackled. White-hot fingers crept across the heavens, searching for a target. A cool gusty wind made the trees creak and groan just as the rain tumbled down. In a matter of seconds, they stood back-to-back, butt naked revelling in the big heavy raindrops.

Clara felt for Nelson's hand and had to shout to be heard. 'I'm going to get the soap and a cloth each. Back in a minute.'

She couldn't hear if Nelson had replied, she'd already run back to the cavern. Returning with soap, rags and one bag of dirty laundry; they bathed then washed.

The thunder was getting further away as the wind and rain weakened. Running back into the cavern, they wrapped themselves in their sun-starched towels and wrung the water out of the clothes into their bathing water container. Nelson swiftly retrieved two of the half-filled buckets of rainwater. At least they had drinking water now. They were used to rationing for survival, and thanks to the heavens they had provisions for three more days.

He was just about to step out of their safe haven when sweeping headlights lit up the tree canopy. Darting backwards, he grabbed the startled Clara and urged her to stand behind the ute. He swiftly dragged their laundry, buckets and anything else obvious to where she was standing before dropping the leafy bark curtain. They silently dressed into the last of their clean, dry clothes and stood completely still in the dark, cool cave waiting and listening.

Ensuring Clara stayed put, Nelson crept along the mud-packed walls towards the opening in the hope of determining the distance of the vehicle. Knowing the road and where the bends and hills were, he determined they had about 30 minutes before the traveller would be upon them. Jogging back to Clara he explained his plan.

'I'm going to sort out the water, you finish wringing our clothes out, lay them on the tray of the Ute then hide like normal, crack the window for fresh air. I'm going to sit in the little dugout near the opening. Nobody will see me. Don't move until the morning.'

'Nelson,' she clutched his hands, 'Sometime back I stole Dad's rifle and some shot. It's rolled up in canvas behind the seat.'

'Clara! That's so dangerous. Your fingerprints are all over it now.'

'No, they're not. I wore socks on my hands.'

'Well, I'm not going to touch it! Let's just hope that nobody discovers it, or us. Hopefully our friend finds us but either way we need to make a decision tomorrow.'

Clara swiped at the tears that were falling freely. 'Sorry, Nelson. I love you. Be careful.'

He squeezed her arm. 'I want to hug you but still don't trust myself. I love you too, Clara. Get some sleep.'

***

Dawn cast an eerie light across the opening of the cavern. Clara cautiously put her head up above the dashboard in the hope she'd see Nelson. To her horror he wasn't where he said he would be. She peered through the rear window praying he'd crept onto the tray and fallen asleep. He hadn't. Panicked, she slipped quietly out of the vehicle and wedged her towel in the door as she pushed it shut. She crept silently along the dirt wall and approached the cold dugout.

As she cautiously peered through the makeshift curtain, she froze in surprise. The bushie and his Blue Heeler were standing with their backs to her, leaning against what looked like Old Mrs D's Willys Jeep. She still could not see Nelson. The Blue Heeler's ears twitched, but he didn't look around. Clara didn't move. Her heart hammered loudly. Eventually, Nelson rounded the knoll carrying a metal detector and pick, sporting a huge grin.

'Sir, this is quite the machine! Look what I've found,' Nelson exclaimed as he approached with an outstretched hand.

Clara could hear their conversation as plain as the breaking day.

'That's a beauty, son! Just think, you'll be able to have one of these for yourself when you're grown up,' the man chuckled warmly. 'Best you go and wake up sleeping beauty.'

Clara raced and hid behind the tailgate. Seeing Nelson's grin elated her mood to the point of being unusually playful. It had been so long since they'd played hide and seek and it just felt so right. Hearing him lightly tap on the front guard then along the door panel, she had to suppress her giggle as he tugged at the trapped towel.

'Clara?' he called out in a hushed voice, 'When I find you, I'm going to spank your bottom.'

She burst out laughing. Bouncing up she ran over and threw her arms around his neck. They hugged each other tightly.

'Come quickly, Clara. Our bushie and pooch are here. We've even got bacon and eggs for breakfast!' Nelson explained excitedly.

She quickly tidied her hair and scrubbed her teeth with her fingers, before tucking in her shirt and followed Nelson out of the cavern.

'Morning Mister,' she held his gaze as she bent down to pat her four-legged friend.

'Clara, trust you slept well. I've had the pleasure of young Nelson here for several hours, hope you're ready for breakfast?'

'Yes please! Mister, did you drive in that storm last night?'

'Ah, yes, I did. Come on, the fire's ready. By the way, there're some chairs in the back of the Jeep, set them up for us, will you?'

The young'uns eagerly worked out the three-legged camping stools and positioned them around the fire, watching in awe as the man cracked half a dozen eggs into the pan alongside a mass of bacon and nicely toasted chunks of bread.

'Can I do anything please, Mister?' Clara asked politely.

'Actually, there is. There's an envelope addressed to you under the front seat. Would you get it please and read it to us men?'

Clara didn't hesitate and ran swiftly to the Jeep. The Blue Heeler bounding along beside with her. She recognised Old Mrs D's handwriting the moment she slid the envelope out from her Bible, and stood with her shoulder's back and chin raised.

In a confident voice, Clara read:

'*My dear surrogate daughter, Clara,*

*Nelson has his own letter, but I want you to read yours out aloud.*

*You cannot help who you fall in love with, I know that only too well. But with a belief in each other and continual support, you will overcome a lot of life's adversities. Trust me on that.*

*Now, Christmas we will meet in Bowen. Your savings—that were stashed away in a most interesting journal—are in the Book of James. Said journal shall remain under safeguard until the timing is appropriate. You must not dwell on it any further. Although I must say you two really would make fine detectives, however; I am relieved you are studying your preferred careers. On that note, your books and studies will be waiting for you when you reach the half-way home. Nelson has the address.*

*You will be responsible for paying your way, as you did with me. Incidentally you pair would also make very good bookkeepers, well done. Your studies are paid for the next year thereby affording you travel money. Be wise. You will also need to find a home.*

*News of your parents will reach you. You have cut the apron strings, now make your own life.*

*I am proud of you and am your trusted friend as you are to me. The kind bush gentleman is our guardian angel, that is for certain.*

*Go with the Grace of God.*

*With love,*

*Old Mrs D.'*

By the time Clara had finished reading, she was almost a blubbering mess.

The bushie handed her a plate piled high with bacon, eggs and bread. 'Clara, everything Old Mrs D wrote is true. I assure you we will all stay in contact and I believe you will become the best darn veterinarian in the north!'

With a watery smile, Clara gripped her plate tightly and whispered loudly, 'Mister, I don't know how to thank you except to say thank you!' Then in a timid voice, she asked, 'Who are you?'

The men replied in unison, 'A guardian angel.'

The bushie winked. 'Eat up now, young'uns, you have a long drive ahead of you. Take the old inland road and follow the timber trails marked on the map. Trade wares for fuel and don't be fooled by inflated prices.'

As Clara helped clean up after breakfast, Nelson explained that the bushie and Old Mrs D had shaken on an agreement which was none of their business. Their trusty old Vauxhall was to stay in the Goldfields along with their secrets and their guardian angel would happily take care of the rifle and ammunition.

Clara felt compelled to give the kind bushie one of her pouches of gold dust. Digging around in the Vauxhall's glovebox she found the cleanest of the two. The dirtiest one went straight into the pocket of her long skirt. There was nothing else of importance so she closed the glovebox for the last time.

While Nelson was repacking the Willys Jeep, Clara distracted the Blue Heeler and consequently gained the man's attention. He approached her with an eyebrow raised and removed his hat.

'Mister, please accept this gift from me,' as she handed him a dusty Royal Blue velvet pouch. 'It weighs half an ounce. Thank you for everything and for being you.'

The Blue Heeler whined softly as the bushie accepted her gift with a broad grin. His soulful eyes filling with tears as he murmured, 'A little bit of kindness goes a long way in this world. Thank you, Clara.'

Rising excitement of their forthcoming adventure gradually replaced a tearful farewell. The bushie's parting words ringing true as the young'uns navigated the unpredictable winding track towards their limitless future.

**The End**

# FEAR the SHATTERED SOULS

Lorie Brink

# Fear The Shattered Souls

Lorie Brink

Lorie Brink

B&W image by Lorie Brink

# Contents

# Prologue

It was always so satisfying when their downcast mouths transformed into watery smiles.

Their welling eyes transformed into steely determination.

Gradual encouragement was all it took for them to start feeling better.

How they eventually accomplished that in its entirety, wasn't her problem.

# Reflections

Kalyani graciously accepted whatever the sufferers could pay, and, whatever she could carry on her aging horse, Judge. The emaciated stallion who ran away with her twelve years earlier. His frame had also done a full circle. Back then, her brazen self would charge three hundred dollars for one hour to listen to someone's sob story. She didn't care where their money came from, they didn't care where she came from, as long as they met somewhere outdoors. Judge helped soothe any anxieties whether a mob of victims turned up, a few, or just one. Most of the money in those days went to Judge, well. . .his vet.

Kalyani's coppery brown skin, high cheek bones and mottled amber eyes weren't the draw card. It was her nose. It hadn't formed properly and instead of protruding; spread like she'd fallen face first into the cruel world.

Shifted from adoption centres, foster homes and communities ever since she could remember, being left to self-defend came as naturally as riding a horse; that talent only discovered at the age of ten.

The head stockman had abuse born into him, was mentally unstable and nasty to two legged bodies. Kalyani had witnessed the depraved behaviour from inside one of the horse stalls hiding from the boss woman who was as evil as her husband, who was eviller than the head stockman.

The scrawny stallion had nuzzled her constantly until she clambered up his back. From thereon, she hid with him whenever she could, in whatever condition she was in. Until the fire.

Then, Kalyani and several other children—their skin colour from matte black to milky white and every shade in between—were returned to their *own people for their own good*.

That decision certainly wasn't for the good of the youngsters. The paedophiliac behaviour continued under the guise of culture and initiation or just plain heinous habit. Another fire. More deaths. More displaced kids.

Again, several of *them under-privileged scrub grubs* were gathered up, rehomed, abused and after the third month of the torturous hell, formed a plan with the older foster kids. It was always a fire. It was the cleanest method. And as they wished, four more damaged adolescents died. Like the never-ending vicious circle, Kalyani was returned to the familiar property. Her saving grace? Judge.

Kalyani had kept a tally of the boys and girls who died by their own hand or by other means. The boys won. The abuse affected them in worse ways than the girls. Suppose for a boy, their only hole down there was for stuff to come out of, not go in.

Several of the abused kids tried to make a noise about it all. Her own people just nodded and said it'd happened to them when they grew up. Kalyani heard that others knew no different. They did. They just used the sick history as an excuse. Live with it, die with it. It just continues.

Government officials turned a blind eye. The social services people disappeared if they intervened. Extenuating consequences for family members of discovered whistleblowers prevented a proper investigation. The abused continued to get abused.

When the voices of the courageous adolescents were ignored, Kalyani, now an older teenager, was determined to make a change in any way she could. A heated conversation between a new ringer and the head stockman, resulted in *take a horse and find somewhere else.* In the middle of the night, the enraged ringer took the order to another level. He hooked up a float, led Judge into the bay, disappeared long enough for Kalyani to hide behind the horse blankets, and drive into the sunrise. After days of travel, they ended up somewhere near the big city. The ringer found a watering hole and was never seen again.

Kalyani and Judge kept to the night shadows, listened to conversations and hatched a plan. Initially, she wanted to start a riot, then thought a more civilised approach would be better. Outside the shire chambers, people demanded to be heard about their inflictions. The ravenous journalists gorged themselves on the drama. Yet, when she muscled her way to the front and exposed the atrocities inflicted upon the vulnerable, the same media people laughed in her face. *Typical half-caste telling lies. Here, take some money and food. Now clear off with that mangy horse. And be quiet. Or else.*

That is how Kalyani and Judge set about a way to help those who needed it more.

Her intense listening skills and peculiar deformity had always made it easier for people to give her things. Money seemed to be the most popular.

Convincing them to kill their monsters?

That was on them.

# The Change

In the ensuing years, word of Kalyani's *cry for help* sessions spread through the communities like the fleas on the mongrel dogs. More recently, the number of attendees had blown her mind. Her age, now somewhere in the late twenties, was more of a survival trophy to see than the flatness of her nose. Judge's greying muzzle had the same attraction, particularly as he now preferred peeled bananas, or rotting apples.

Until now, any resultant deaths became apparent after she'd long gone. Kalyani sensed her luck was running out because the distance between her and the decaying monsters was getting shorter. At the last three gatherings there were more kids too old for foster homes than there were younger ones who turned up. They were eager to establish chapters. Enlist victims. Go international. Go underground. Prove that the *dark web* had more than one definition.

Technology was foreign to her. Cold. Impersonal. Kalyani listened encouragingly. Yet, it was not up to her how the victims helped themselves to feel better.

One older female had *followed* Kalyani's three recent sessions, carrying her own firestick. As if that wasn't the only thing that bugged Kalyani. The woman's repeated story just didn't gel and Kalyani believed had never been abused in her life. In fact, Kalyani suspected the bitch probably did the abusing simply by the way she had manipulated those sessions.

Tonight's gathering had been particularly awkward.

Her knowledge of government, how a whitey had failed the people and a black fella had gotten into running the show, and now everything was going to be good for her people; it all stank. The abused had all heard it, all before, from all colours. Even ones with slanted eyes or a red dot on their forehead. This creamy bitch told them that the black fella was moving into the whitey's house, the exact town it was located in, and, she was going to be there for the handing over of the keys. She even promised that she would help the mob. She almost bragged that she was going to start right there and then. She did not extend an invite to Kalyani.

But before this thing had latched onto the white bawling sixteen-year-old male, he had told the group of a predator who wore different clothes and sometimes spoke in different voices. As the wave of distrust crashed over them, the sufferers clammed up. Nobody paid. Nobody cried for help. They just cried from frustration, and utter demoralisation. They got swallowed up in the loveless prickly scrub.

Bad juju dressed as a woman supported the blubbering deranged teenager, and held up the firestick, blocking Kalyani's path.

'You won't remember me. You were too young, Kalyani. None of these awful things were meant to happen to you or any of youse. I had to go back to my own people because. . .'

'I don't care for your history or excuses. None of it.' Kalyani spat bloody phlegm at the woman's feet. 'You don't even know what colour you are. Best you look after that white fella. He's messed up in the head and all that is on you and your people.'

'I'm trying to warn you. You have to be careful. They're looking for you.'

'Nah. Bet you probably dobbed me in. Best you leave now.'

'Here me out first. There are a lot of dead monsters in your wake, you stupid woman. You can't go around killing people because of what they did.'

'What they did? You make it sound like it was nothing. Besides, I haven't laid a hand on anyone. How victims deal with their demons is not my problem.'

'Kalyani! You encouraged them!'

'Prove it.'

The sobbing lad urinated against the woman's leg.

'Great,' she muttered.

'Yep, the result of your so-called help! He needs a mental hospital, you the stupid woman,' Kalyani hurled loudly.

'We can work together . . . I tried to help and I failed. But I'm older now and have . . .'

'I don't care about you, but that boy needs help. Go away,' and pointed angrily over the woman's shoulder.

Kalyani waited until the crickets began their chirping sonata. It was time for her and Judge to leave without a trace. Only Judge ate dinner. Only Judge had eaten the last several meals. Under the milky way, Judge kept to the tree line along the bulldust riddled track while Kalyani plotted her last hurrah astride his back. Haunted by her own demons and a silent killer eating her from the inside, there was one thing left for her to do. Visit the black fella who was running the show. She reckoned she knew which black fella it was too.

## VEHEMENCE

When she was little, he had always said he would rule their country. He had also taught her and her brothers and sisters how to tell stories through words marked on paper or into the dirt with a sharp stick. They cried if they got the story wrong. They cried if they got the story right. He told them that he would fix things so nobody would cry anymore. He told them that all the boys and girls would be loved. He lied.

# The Power Of Thought

Eleven sunrises later, with drying bloodied spittle staining her shirt and pants, Kalyani's laboured breath matched Judge's. Using her knees to hold her aloft, she twisted around and waved weakly. Walking behind her in straggled rows on the lush green grass, a dusty coloured forlorn mob returned her wave. In front of them all; clean, wide steps leading to the huge new home of the man running the show.

The crowd waiting to witness history parted in fear. Or dread. Or guilt. Or God forbid, depravity. Kalyani and Judge didn't care. They nosed their way into the faces of the camera people.

'Get away,' they shrieked. 'You're not allowed here.'

Judge wrapped his mouth around a fuzzy microphone and flung his head back. Catching it awkwardly, the handle clipped Kalyani on the chin. Her cuss filled the large speakers. The onlookers gasped and moved further away as she teetered and spat another clot of dark blood. Her mob rushed the crowd.

The huge timber doors flung open and there he stood. The one who lied. Beside him, a pallid man. His look of scorn dripped like a soiled nappy.

'You are trespassing,' he yelled. 'Go back to wherever you came from.'

The juju woman strode alongside the black fella and stood beside him at the edge of the steps. She glared at Kalyani. Nudged her counterpart in the ribcage.

'What you mob doing here?' he hollered.

Kalyani tapped the fuzz. Everyone fell silent except Judge, who whinnied loudly. 'Long time back, you learnt me to read. You hurt me, me sisters and me brothers. We know you. We know you like boys and girls.'

She coughed, slid off Judge and sat in his shadow. His weary legs folded beside her. She laid her head against his rib cage and spoke again.

'You lie to us back then. You lie to all us now. You lie to everyone. Are youse mob all paedos? How many of you do it because it was done to you? Blacks, whites, browns, creamies? All us have been done. You see us? All us different colours? Bubs, toddlers, all the way to teenagers. Why you think so many of us don't care? Hate? Kill? Commit suicide? You stole our dignity.'

Her mob yelled out their disgusted opinions, until Kalyani pointed at the familiar woman. The monotonous loud ascending whistle of an Eastern Koel amplified her inner rage.

'And you? Do you select the prey for your mob? When will it stop? How many of us must keep suffering? The truth has to come out. You're in power. You're all...'

Kalyani's voice failed as a racking cough stole her energy. Judge snorted painfully and laid his head on the grass, nibbled, then sighed exhaustedly. Everyone watched as his enlarged heart slowed. Kalyani curled her bony frame into his, both hands feebly holding onto the handset.

'If paedo's are running this land, what. . .hope. . .have. . .we. . .got?'

The microphone tumbled out of her hand. Its pitiful squeal penetrating the air as it hit the ground.

Kalyani's head lolled into Judge's ear. 'We did it, Judge. . .I die with you, but our. . .spirit. . .live. . .on.'

# The Devil Is In The Details

Kalyani woke up in a large, bright room with floor to ceiling windows. Beyond, a view overlooking the ocean. The sunflower covered doona complimented the terracotta-coloured walls. Her throat ached. Her eyes stung. Blood filled tubes and heavy wires protruded out of her skeletal frame. The blip of the heart monitor soft, but loud. Her only free skinny wrist, handcuffed to the bed rail.

'Ah, you're awake.' A portly quarter-caste wearing blue scrubs let her suck on a water-soaked facecloth, then sat with a clipboard on his lap facing her. 'Sorry to tell you the bad news first, but we couldn't save your horse. We reckoned he was over twenty years old! You served him well.'

Tears trickled down Kalyani's cheeks. Eventually, she managed to croak, 'Judge saved me.'

'You didn't make the newspaper if that was your hope, but I heard you speak at the gathering. You pick your audience as to how you speak. Who educated you?'

Kalyani reflected on the lessons she'd been dealt. 'Several people, several books. What about you?'

'Not here for a social visit. Any idea how many kids you've talked to?'

'Nuh. I no talk to you without another person witness. But you tell me good news.'

'Only that your horse was taken away by your people. . .'

'My people? What are you?'

'Not here to talk about me, but you probably caused more trouble over the last three months than you did your whole life.'

'What?'

'Yep. You one of the lucky ones.'

Kalyani scoffed. 'Handcuffed to a bed, half dead and you call me lucky.'

The nurse offered her more water. 'You been on life support in a safe place. They brought you out of a coma yesterday and said you wake up by yourself today. We're sort of like outlaws in this place. A lot of foot soldiers, wardens, that's what I am, and leaders.'

'Why didn't they just let me die with Judge?'

'The boss wanted to be able to talk to you sometime.'

'Sometime? What colour is he now?'

'It's a woman and she's a creamy.' The nurse flipped up a picture.

Kalyani scoffed. 'Where's the white boy she stole?'

'Safe.'

'Like I'm important?'

At that moment, the woman swept into the room. Her long turquoise jacket flaring outwards over a baggy white pantsuit. Pitch black hair plastered her skull, face made up like it could be used a glowstick. Her voice was different. More refined.

'Thank you, Ginee, you can stay.'

She then looked at Kalyani and spoke quietly. 'While you've been sleeping, several government departments were overrun by people with revenge on their minds. Their rampant rage and urgency flushed out the sickos, named and shamed the monsters, ravaged the media and this country has been turned on its head. What's worse, you've exposed factions that weren't ready.'

Kalyani's eyes watered. A tiny smile played about her insipid mouth.

'Your name is still whispered through the ghost gums. And that horse of yours? Pity he wasn't put into stud when you got him good and fat. Nonetheless, I'm momentarily undecided what to do with you now that you're awake, so we'll just talk . . .'

'I don't get it,' Kalyani murmured, drawing in the pumped air until her lungs ached.

'Well, nearly everyone who heard you say your piece certainly got it. And now, we all have to be careful. Everyone who knows, knows. And those who are involved have very different contacts to the likes of you and me.'

'So?'

'It all comes down to money. Oh, and consequences. They are the absolute cruellest to accept. No, *comprehend*, a far better word.' The woman jammed her fists on her hips. 'Consequences are the absolutely cruellest to comprehend. You see, your supporters and their families were discovered, ostracised, then rounded up by their so-called friends, and since shut up.'

'Jail or hospital?'

'Neither. Besides, the damage you caused has spread beyond the borders of this country.'

The woman casually toyed with the life-monitoring wires. Her fascination with the blood filtering through the tubes kept her busy for several minutes. Suddenly, she threw her head back in anger.

'Do you realise the damage you have caused to government funding, international relations, economics, educational facilities? I could go on, but you're intelligent enough to know what I'm talking about.'

'So what? These damages you talk about all get fixed at the next election. The hush up money is churned out at the Mint. The lists are filed away in a never-to-be-seen filing cabinet. They're kept hidden, the demeaning behaviour just goes on. Backroom parties aren't necessarily categorised for political debates. And the media manipulators are involved. . .' Kalyani gasped as the air was abruptly cut from oxygen tube.

'You actually know too much. Even worse, you have exposed the very people we were trying to keep hidden because another plot was already in play.'

'And. . .you. . .are. . .who?'

The woman squeezed the ventilator tube with every word she uttered. 'The. One. To. Take. This. To. A. Whole. New. Level.'

Kalyani forced out her reply. 'How?'

An evil grin parted the neon painted mouth. 'We will finally get away with the perfect murder all because of you!'

Ginee clapped his hands. Startled, the woman spun around, pulled a small gun from out of nowhere and shot him between the eyes. She then yanked out the oxygen tubes as if nothing had happened.

'Mark my words, none of what you did will be in vain.'

Kalyani's last words were barely audible. 'The. . .boy?'

'My vice president of the Kalyani Chapter. Goodbye girl. This machine has kept you alive for long enough.'

**The End**

# INHERITED OBSESSIONS

# Inherited Obsessions

Lorie Brink

Lorie Brink

B&W image by Lorie Brink

# Contents

# 1977
# Butterflies

Bored with the debate about mysterious deaths of people long before her parents were even born, Marnie disappeared up the flight of stairs. She had way better things to do. And having the entire storey to herself, she skipped all the way into her bedroom. Besides, today was meant to be a happy day, not listen to an argument between Jarrod (her sixteen-year-old brother) and mother (Leanna), with her father (Kevan) always being the referee.

The eleven-year-old tucked in some loose pages and carefully closed the antique anthology, puffed out her cheeks then stared into her open wardrobe. Hanging separately to her other clothes, the outfit of choice for the event filled afternoon; her deep mauve flower-girl dress, matching shoes and a camphor-smelly apple green shawl with its weighty, aged yellow trim. Not even her mother knew what she had chosen to wear, and nobody knew she'd snuck into the attic. The creaky stairs that led off the western wing had intrigued her as soon as she could walk. Marnie had hoped there would be some dress-up costumes stashed away, after all, some ancient relative had been involved with the arts in Great Britain, and she had been right. She just hoped she wouldn't get into trouble today.

Patting the tummy butterflies, it was time to get dressed, even though the shawl made her feel like she was boiling. Marnie wrapped her treasured book in its tatty velvet cover and hoped the old man who guarded the stage would still be alive. She made her family call to her three times before a melodramatic entrance into the grand ballroom.

'Ta-da!'

'Oh, you're not!' Jarrod chided and faked a spew. 'It's only the annual entertainment for homeless at the soup kitchen, not some formal affair in the glamour strip of Sydney!'

'It's my turn to shine,' she giggled, raced over and tickled him. 'Besides, since forever I had to listen to you playing on the marimba, so now it's your turn to listen to me tell a story.'

He affectionately tucked a stray ringlet behind her ear, knowing how his little sister desperately wanted to grow long hair, yet her walnut mop kept producing unconquered curls.

'You will be there, won't you?' she blurted out.

'The only time I won't attend a special occasion of yours is if someone we know is dead.' Jarrod feigned a collapse.

'Hey! That's my saying. Get your own.'

While their kids were laughing and chasing each other through the billiards room, conservatory, library and other entertainment areas of the sprawling ground floor, Leanna stated quietly, 'You know which story our bookworm is talking about, don't you?'

'Her outfit pretty much gave it away.' Kevan looked at his childhood sweetheart with concern. 'Did you know she'd been in the attic?'

'Nope. I thought we were keeping our suite locked to prevent that! Anyway, when was the last time you went through those old things?'

'Three months ago, on dad's heavenly birthday. I didn't open the old shipping trunks, but I swapped out the mothballs in all the boxes. . . just can't bring myself to throwing anything out!'

'My sweet, sentimental fool whose generation got more looks and brains than theatrics. Except for memorising and reciting silly tales.'

'You've got a nerve! Your side were also on stage. Anyway, it's a thought-provoking story. Even Jarrod talked about it while we were tinkering in the shed trying to clean up that old letter opener.' Kevan smirked. 'It's funny how we all remember only one story from that archaic collection.'

'Humph. Only because it's been constantly repeated!'

'Bookworms yearn for the conclusion of a cliffhanger. And treasures, witches and unexplained deaths seem to be a topic of conversation lately. Is it because they're just a memory now?' Kevan threw his hands in the air. 'Today's radio show even mentioned a lost hair pin and huge diamond! Probably not connected, but how uncanny is that? Pity Marnie missed it! But come on, Leanna, you won't flex just a little bit?'

Rolling her eyes, 'It's just a story. A fairy tale!'

'Fine. I don't expect you to get it, so let's just agree to disagree? Remember, Marnie's the star today.'

Leanna huffed. 'Who has inherited your obsession.'

'About that,' Kevan cleared his throat. 'You need to show some interest in your son's entry for the Days of Yore blacksmith competition. And cheer up!'

Their tête-à-tête abruptly ended as the car horn tooted thrice, followed by a pair of fun-loving voices loudly encouraging them to get a move on.

The usual singalong journey wasn't as uplifting. Exasperated, Leanna exhaled noisily the minute they parked.

'What's up?' Kevan said.

'I left the bundle of tea-towels.'

'Good. We get out of cleaning up,' Jarrod mumbled.

Marnie giggled, leant over the bench seat and rested her hand upon her father's cheek. 'I'm really happy you're home Daddy.'

'So am I. Now, come along, the star can't be late for the show!'

'Try and get front row seats!' Marnie called over her shoulder and raced to a group of her schoolfriends. The smallest of the bunch, Zessi, hugged her tightly. 'You look so regal, Miss Marnie, you could fly like an eagle!'

'And you will be a famous poet one day, Zessi!'

Giggling, the girls ran towards the hall, only to be stopped by an older boy blocking the doorway. Hands on hips.

'Gidday Mar, Zes,'

'Hello Damon,' the girls answered shyly.

'You both look lovely. I'll escort you inside.'

He looped their arms through his and paraded the pair through the milling crowd.

'Break a leg, Mar. I'm going to find that crazy brother of yours.'

The girls swooned and gazed after his disappearing back. 'He's such a gentleman,' Zessi said.

Marnie smiled at her best friend. 'One day he'll see you for the beauty you are.'

They hugged. 'Good luck, Miss Marnie, really hope you don't break a leg!'

She watched Zessi get swallowed up by the throng, then raced towards the dressing rooms.

# Story Time

The inner-city's soup kitchen swelled with far too many homeless, the usual freeloaders, and a heartwarming gathering of volunteers during the afternoon's varied entertainment. Enjoyment was amplified with poetry recitals, mini stage plays, and a combined performance of the local ballet school waltzing to music played by the junior school's orchestra. Being the Head Girl, Marnie Ward was the final act.

Kevan remained seated between the quarrelsome duo. Jarrod nudged his father and pointed towards the stage.

'I see the old boy is still kicking. Reckon this must be his seventh, no, eighth year in a row?'

They looked at the age-weary man typically settled in the closest chair to the stage, yet the furthest from any other person. The same shabby green blanket hugging his bony body.

'Even longer than that. More importantly, stop butting heads with your mother.'

Just then, Leanna tapped Kevan's knee and murmured into his ear. 'Look! He's still alive. . . Jarrod's biggest supporter is going to get a surprise this year but his blanket is getting really threadbare now.' Leanna blinked away tears. 'It's going to be an awful winter this year, how about we offer him the old greenhouse?'

Kevan's reply was lost. Marnie pushed the ornate reading chair centre stage, sat gracefully with her legs together at a gentle angle. Silence befell the audience when the emcee, dressed as a butler, handed her the microphone, bowed and walked backwards until he disappeared behind the faux wings. All eyes fell on Marnie who waved her right hand regally.

'Ahem. Why doesn't the Queen wave with this hand?' she asked with a-plum-in-her-mouth accent.

Sniggers filled the hall, until a crackly old voice closest to the stage called out, 'Dunno. Why?'

'Oh,' Marnie replied haughtily, 'because it is mine!'

Her parents stared at each other guffawing loudly. Jarrod's belly laugh competed with his rhythmic thigh slapping. The old man performed a seated jig and contributed to the raucous appreciation.

In a tone sprinkled with mischief; Marnie's sweet, innocent voice hushed her audience. 'Please get comfortable. I am going to recite my absolute favourite story written a very, very long time ago by A Non. It isn't a long story, but it does raise a lot of questions. The author's name is top of my list.' She paused dramatically. 'Hmm, anonymous or a non de plume?'

Marnie blew three kisses to her family, smiled sweetly at the old man and gave him a cute little wave.

'Let's begin.'

***'The Mystical Hand Forged Copper Hair Pin***

*Under the flickering light from the soy wax candle, a jewel-studded, burgundy painted long fingernail sparkled down the list of candidates. Two special names were who she was looking for. Two sons of aristocratic standing of whom befitted an illicit transaction. Ox Cart Annie straightened her hair piece as she wriggled her matronly posterior towards the edge of the antique solid wooden chair, mimicking its groaning complaint. Her commissioned forest green and gold-gilded mantelet jutting like a decorated horse's hindquarter. Dramatic thespian furniture as stagnant as the heavy burgundy curtains shielded the dilapidated stage. At last! A dollop of dripping wax fell beside each of the unsuspecting progenies.*

*Lifting her nose into the air, the familiar whiff of the street urchin drifted cautiously through the open trapdoor beside her desk.*

*'A message, me lady,' the timid voice ventured. 'Meet at midnight behind The Twisted Goblet...'*

*Silence befell the disused stage pit.*

*'When?' Her shrill voice clashed with the elegance of her deep violet gown.*

*A muffled yawp, then silence.*

*Ox Cart Annie swept her boot-clad foot across the lever slamming the trapdoor shut. With a calmness paradoxical to the situation, she fan-folded the furtive list and tucked it into the treasured garment's secret pocket. Stale dusty particles wafted lazily in her wake. Her shadow loomed until it too was engulfed by the inky darkness behind the velvet drapes. Satiny flounces swished against the lumber half wall for eleven paces. Invoking the spirits, she removed her amulet freeing grizzled black hair to cascade down her broad ridge.*

*Shimmying into the comforting recess, hair pin in mouth, she intertwined the priceless curved copper clip through the cotton corsetry folded between her heaving bosoms. Their entrapment threatened to burst their bounds. The metallic taste compelled her to swallow feverishly. Yellowed teeth protruded from burgundy painted lips as she gently removed her unsheathed weapon and gripped it firmly between her meaty hands. With expelled rancid breath, Ox Cart Annie cast forth her dancing flame spell.*

*The heavy thud of the trapdoor followed by muffled grunts and groans filtered through the dank air. Someone wrestled their way upwards. The sheer presence of strangers executed malevolence. Along with ancestral tones, the concurrent masculine conversation made her quiver.*

*'Nuffin but a madly flickerin' candle. The witch, she be gone.'*

*'Any sign of the list?'*

*'Nay but twigs and small bones, but there be a right real pong that closes off ya throat.'*

*'Oi, come back ya scrawny wretch...blast it all to hell, the ruddy brat's done a runner!'*

*'P'raps I look around for a wee while?'*

*Clanging bells and echoed cries of 'fire' rose and fell like the cacophony of a rehearsing orchestra.*

*'We gotta be gone too. Quick! Follow me.'*

*No response was heard.*

*Something fluttered across the bloated flesh beneath Ox Cart Annie's chin before a large gloved hand sealed her mouth.*

*A hairy whisper encased her left ear. 'The list for the child.'*

*Thrashing her head from side to side, she engaged the hair pin in a frenzied attack desperately seeking the lithe body. An indescribable force thrust her into the open. Dark energy wrung her wrists. Possessed, her now empty hands clasped together behind her back ruptured the fabric across her bodice.*

*Devilishly howled words echoed through the drapes. 'Seeketh what belongeth.'*

*Her mouth was free. In a voice louder than a foghorn in treacherous seas, commanded, 'None shall be. I release you forthwith.'*

*A shaft of malicious light coincided with the hefty woman's buckled knees. The sea roared in her ears. Piquant woodsy smoke destroyed any hope of survivable air as its fumes charred her facial orifices.*

*Suddenly, a wet small hand patted her mouth.*

*'Mammy. Fire! Fire!'*

*With the garment and gown twisted together, Ox Cart Annie's legs failed. She fumbled blindly around her buxom femininity and grimaced as the copper gouged the soft flesh. With her usual calmness, eventually shrugged free of her heritage.*

*Clasping the hand, she murmured. 'Sweet child, let me hear the rune. Quickly now.'*

*'Yes, Mammy. Stowaway and never let the papyrus see day. They must pay or rue the day. The cloak me worth, the copper our right from birth.' Nose to nose, the child continued tearfully, 'Your turn.'*

*'Together the pieces be, or apart, forever you own my heart. Run away, stowaway, we will meet another day.'*

*Their mingled voices whispered the last promise. 'Only when it's safe.'*

*Allegiance and adoration reflected in their watery eyes as eager flames crawled up the curtains. The child artfully wove the clip and further hitched the britches. Forlorn, yet resourceful, folded the mantelet and merged with the thickening grey-black smoke.*

*The End.'*

# Perpetuation

Wonderfully loud accolades filled the hall as Marnie gleefully removed the shawl and left it folded on the chair. She pushed through the closing curtains and leapt into her family's embrace.

Hidden from view, the old man danced slowly towards his prize and inhaled the tainted mustiness of the priceless cashmere shawl. Contained within his ancient green protector, an old leather journal. Atop, the hand forged copper clip encased by a shakily handwritten note. He cast his farewell, and crossed his heart.

Sweet child, safekeep all with the copper hair pin.
Best kept a secret 'til ye have grandchildren.
Nurture only thine thespian craft.
O'er time, no names to the list added be,
An oath from the best of Ox Cart Annie.
A Non lives forever in ye heart.

Marnie escaped the cleaning up duties and snuck backstage to discover her father and Jarrod already there, having an intense discussion. Racing over, she swooped onto the green fabric.

'The old man! Where is he?' Then she looked more closely, 'This is similar to the mantelet! Could it be?'

'Uh, you need to read this,' her father spoke gently and pressed the note into her hands.

Her eyes widened, refolded it and tucked it down the front of her dress then feigned a shock at what he held in his other hand. 'That's the clip! Dad, we gotta go. I think I know where the hair pin is.'

'So do we,' Jarrod winked and held out the journal. 'We think this belongs to you too.'

'Have you read any of it?' she challenged, now making the front of her dress bulge.

'No.'

'There you all are!' Mother stormed across the stage. 'What's going on here?'

The three of them stuttered and stammered, until eventually Jarrod wrapped his sister in the old garment.

On cue, Father said, 'The old man needed something warmer, so we traded. I feel good that he's got the shawl.'

'Yes, winter will be here before we know it, Mum.'

'And just what is down the front of your dress, young lady?'

Jarrod nudged Marnie gently. Being the sweet child, reluctantly handed over her gifts. She watched in horror as her mother read the note, flicked through the journal then shoved it, and the clip down the front of her own dress.

'Kevan, we need to leave right now.'

They made it home in record time. The silent grandeur of the century-old sprawling manor wove its spell the moment the attic window came into view, then the outline of the oversized mannequin's head. Lastly, adorning the white window box, trailing pink roses.

Breathlessly, Leanna said, 'Park near the old service wing.'

Once inside, her voice held an air of mystery mingled with relief. 'I had hoped we would be a memory before you kids discovered the secret.' She ran her fingers through Marnie's curls and smiled. 'I was under oath unless something changed, which happened today! You need to pay heed to the wise words of my old man, sweet child.'

'You knew all along?' Kevan's tone as bewildered as the looks on their children's faces.

'Yes. I've kept this secret since Marnie's age, Kevan, and longer still shall it be kept. My father had to be estranged for everyone's safety. That's why we have always attended the soup kitchen from our dating days at school.'

Leanna fell in love with his boyish dumbfounded look all over again.

'The story. . . it's all true?' Marnie whispered.

'Not all of it, no. Ox Cart Annie was beautiful, and you have similar curls!' Leanna grinned, slowly casted her glistening eyes over the men in her life. 'Now, you pair, you have been trying to remove layers of copper carbonate. Not rust. Jarrod, I will take the so-called letter opener and you had better have forged a Damascus steel blade if you're going to win this competition.'

He stared at his mother. 'You also know what that is?'

'And more.' She performed a balestra towards an old Victorian oak bookcase, reached forwards and locked the stained-glass doors. With a hard shove, the piece of furniture slid sideways revealing stairs to an underground room. 'You'll need knight's armour if you're going to win. Seek your preferred costume! I'm going to take the tea-towels to the soup kitchen. Have whatever you like to eat. I'll be back later.'

An invisible magnet drew father and children downwards. Leanna sneezed, sniffed twice and caught the whiff of stale smoke, and sneezed again.

'But Mum! When are you going to tell us more?' Marnie yelled from deep within the newfound playroom.

With her spellbound family playing dress-up, Leanna walked away clutching the journal and hair pin, whispering, 'Only when it's safe.'

Much later that night, the old man crept out of the shed and stuck to the shadows. The breathless night giving way to summer's door. He took one last look at the stately old home and murmured. 'Keep safe, o' daughter o' mine, and keep everything safe.

Rustling leaves made him stall his journey. 'Stay on your own path, wayward one,' he commanded firmly.

'Nay, Papa, let me talk with you.'

Father and daughter hugged and wept. Their wordless bond etched deep into their souls.

Eventually, Leanna said, 'The prime minister's office has written seeking information about my grandparents. This is much earlier than expected.'

'It is nothing to be concerned about. A situation will arise and it shall be forgotten. I must go, sweet child.'

'Papa, you mumbled something before. Can you come inside? See your home again? Sit at the head of the dining table . . .?'

He hushed his weeping daughter. 'No. Just keep safe, o' daughter o' mine, and keep everything safe.'

'Those are your last wishes?'

'No. These are so listen carefully. Seal the attic. Marnie can only learn of the truth when she's stopped playing the actress, or has a more sensible role.'

'Hope I'm still alive to see that!'

'As do I. I'll watch over Jarrod until I can't, but I can see he's already on his own path of keeping an ancient craft alive. Let him be the man he wants to be. He will always look out for his little sister. That's one tradition that will change.' His voice cracked. 'Well, that's what I hope with all my heart.'

Leanna watched her father's shoulders shake at the age-old regretful sorrow of him unable to protect those closest to his heart. Agonised tears flowed down her own cheeks at the awful childhood memory of seeing her mother and aunt hanging from the rail bridge. Terrifyingly, women had always been the keepers of the journal up until that particular tragedy.

The old man sobered first. 'You've grown into a remarkable woman and are a wonderful mother, Leanna. But we're flirting with danger now. I urge you to hide the journal well, then take Kevan and Marnie and get out of town.'

Leanna tapped the front of her dress. 'But why? I've flicked through the pages. Our names aren't on it!'

'I don't believe you have read the writings on all the pages?'

'That is true.'

'Nevertheless, the journal is where it belongs. Bury the blasted thing if you have to. Now, sweet child,' he gathered her into his frail embrace, 'go home to your family.'

'But what about you, Papa?'

'My time will come. The waterways shall be my grave, the skies my soul's resting place.'

He put his hands over her eyes, kissed her forehead. 'Go now. A Non lives forever in ye heart.'

Before Leanna could wipe the tear that slid slowly down her face, the old man took a step backwards and simply disappeared.

Leanna sank against the nearest tree trunk. Under the dim glow of her penlight torch, she fanned the pages from the right to left. Fear stabbed her in the heart. Fighting back the tears, she fled like a gazelle. Darting this way and that, in case she was already in the crosshairs.

# Warden Of Cruel Mercy

Panicked, Leanna crept through the staff's entrance and scaled the staircase nimbly. Her feet padded lightly on the carpeted timber until she stepped out onto the wing of Jarrod's suite. It was aglow with every mode of light available. Her darling son sat in front of the large draftsman's board. With firm graceful strokes, The Longford Sword came alive on the canvas. In typical fashion, he drew the design repeatedly. By the time he was in his forge, he knew the weapon intimately.

Her father's words jolted her into action. With body pressed along the wall, she finally slid open the door to the next stairwell. Upwards she crept, until eventually the familiar tickle of excitement pressed her onwards. Deliberately missing the first timber step because of its screaming creak, she climbed the rest of the staircase in the same manner she did as a kid. Hands and knees, beside the still wobbly iron balustrade.

A slither of light shone through the cracks of the staircase. She had to hurry. Kevan would soon be looking for her. Inside the attic, the lure of the forbidden trunks was too strong to ignore. Especially the largest one. It had always been her favourite. Beside it, the left wrist of the mannequin still hung limply, and inside that was the handkerchief that housed the key. As soon as the ancient key hit her palm, her skin tingled.

Talking softly to each trunk, she eventually sat before her personal favourite. Lifting its lid, she squealed silently. The ethanol-filled specimen jar of ancient creatures still captivated her interest. Except the ones with eyes. Those freaked her out. Leanna tapped the lid of the most important jar. Daring to lift it out, she admired the perfectly preserved long sinewy tendons trailing behind the digit. Swiftly returning the trunk to its original status, the key to its hiding place, her poise stiffened as the first step screamed in protest.

'Who is in the attic?' Kevan demanded.

'It's me, Kevan, I'm on my way down now.'

Hide the journal! Her mind screamed. Leanna returned the dead stare of the mannequin. Its midriff spiked into a timber block sitting atop an old wooden chair.

'Leanna?' Kevan stepped into the room just as Leanna patted the fibreglass head.

'Right, that's all tidied up now.'

'What's a woman like you doing in a place like this?' he said.

'Saying my goodbyes. You ought to as well.'

'Another time, yet I must say, it's oddly reassuring that you're not planning on throwing anything out!'

'That'll be up to the kids.'

Encouraged by her descent, he asked the dreaded question. 'What's really going on, Leanna?'

In a quiet voice she levelled with him.

Startled, 'And what of Jarrod?'

'He's a sensible teenager with a determination akin to his blades. Old Barnard and staff will make sure he's well fed and well behaved.'

'And Zessi? The school?'

'It'll all work out. Once Marnie has recovered...'

'Recovered? What on earth are you going to do?'

'She won't remember a thing, except being an overnight sensation in the acting world. Then we'll come home.'

'When do you anticipate that will be? I do have a job you know.'

Leanna's look of utter derision encouraged Kevan to clamp his mouth shut. He watched his wife dash off to the suitcase closet then disappear down their hallway. He glanced up at the attic door, pursed his lips and deliberately missed the first two stairs.

***

Jarrod returned to his suite, extinguished the lights and tousled up the bedsheets. Just in case his parents did come to bid adieu, it would be better if at least he pretended to be asleep. His mind abuzz with adrenaline. At long last, he could implement his plan without the prying eyes of a dear little sister.

# Crucible Of Dreams

Blueprints of the stately manor covered the antique twelve-seater dining table. Drafting board offset to the buffet bar, alterations complete, Jarrod sighed heavily and rested his socked feet on the nearest seat. He had no idea about stonemasonry or how to construct buildings. The set of encyclopedias strewn across the floor gaped back at him with the same ignorance.

'Master Jarrod?'

'Ah, Barnard! Your timing is impeccable. Don't suppose you know how this place was built do you?'

'Only the fifty-year old kitchen. But you have more pressing matters right now.'

'Oh? What is that?'

'A visitor who made his own way into the drawing room.'

'Odd?'

'No, he grew up here and has already requested tea.'

Jarrod triple-jumped the books, skated through the grand ballroom and performed a fencing lunge as he entered the room.

'Whoa, steady on young fella!' a raspy voice called out from beside the fireplace.

'You! Who are you?' Jarrod strode over; hand extended.

'Truth be known, your grandfather. Your parents do not know I am here and it is best we keep it that way.'

'Yes, sir . . . Pops? Can I call you that?'

'That sounds nice.'

Barnard announced tea time, poured three cups and promptly sat down. 'A few truths for you, young man. I'm a distant relative who is not here as your guardian. This old fart will take on that role. Like I told you two weeks ago, the rest of your family will return when the time is right.'

He pointed towards the oldest painting of an aristocrat and described how the jolly old fellow was apparently the bastard son of a Spanish duke in the late 1600s. With the handiwork of a clever scribe and a bag of silver to claim the birthright, led the way for an incestuous marriage. Afterwards, natural attrition and the benefits of the family name flowed like a waterfall. That was, until a wayward offspring of the bloodline decided it was easier to make acquisitions through illegal gambling dens. Roots of the family tree crept into many crevices. Along with the adventure came the peril. Barnard's grin disappeared behind the lip of this tea cup.

The old man arose and traced the wrought ironwork of the mantlepiece above the fireplace. His eyes tunnelled into Jarrod's soul. Eventually, said, 'This skillset has been in my family for eons. I can teach you about that and how to ride a horse.'

'Can you tell me more about this hand forged copper hair pin?'

'No. I simply cannot.'

'The journal then?'

Barnard made a show of stacking the teacups. 'Master Jarrod, perhaps Pops can help with your earlier question about construction of this stately home?'

The elderly men exchanged glances.

Barnard posed a question as he excused himself from the room. 'What is it you seek, young man?'

'I want to live in two centuries. Medieval times from sunset to sunrise, in current times until twilight. That's my ideal dream. But first, the suites in this home need a renovation. I want Marnie to live on the fourth storey so she can play in her beloved attic. Mum and Dad can be totally self-sufficient on the third storey. Below that, my own museum and science lab.'

'Bloody 'ell,' Pops stated flatly, 'So much for an easy retirement!'

Jarrod indicated over his shoulder. 'If you care to accompany me in the dining room, I'll show my plans for the old barn, secret room and the estate.'

He then bellowed towards the kitchen, 'Barnard, we'll have supper in the conservatory. Join us, won't you?'

'Quite the man of the house . . .'

'Hey, the oldies never woke me before they left. They haven't penned me a note or sent a postcard. I know not where Marnie ended up. So yes, I am the man of the house. Ultimately I wish to be known as a Knight, but I have a lot to do before then.'

In the dining room, he guided the old man through a makeshift path between the encyclopedias. Stood in front of the drafting board and presented his plan.

'Where would you like to spend eternity, Pops?'

'Amid the nest of white swans.'

Jarrod smirked. 'I'll need a moat first.'

'We have a lot to do before that happens. First, some ground rules. Number one: there are some items that need to be removed from the attic, and there are some items that are never to be touched . . .'

'Fear not, old man. I hate it up there.'

'Good. Number two: you'll need to build a science lab. Number three: the PM's office was sniffing around the heritage of your home.'

'Eh? That's a bit odd.'

'Not really, given this place is over a century old. It's a valuable piece of dirt in the big picture. If it's worth anything, someone will always try and pull the carpet out from under you. Remember that, Jarrod.'

'Okay. Is that why Mum and Dad left with Marnie in the middle of the night?'

'No. That mystery will unfurl itself in good time.'

Jarrod shrugged. 'Fine. What's the third rule then?

'Don't discuss the news with anybody over the telephone.'

Confused, Jarrod turned up his nose. 'That doesn't make sense.'

'It will. Now, rule number four, and probably the most important one for you; create a future and forget about the dramas of the past.'

'Too easy, mate. I'm not one for fairy tales . . . unless it's about blacksmiths!'

The old man ruffled his grandson's head affectionately.

# 1984

# Zessi

Waves of curling mist broke with the march of the cloaked doctor leading a party of jacketed nurses. Milky moonlight glinted off the steel blade swinging off his roped belt. They chanted to a sanitised beat.

*Left, right, left, right, we receive our prize tonight. A vessel to nurture, a gift of life in the future.*

Looking down onto herself, Zessi watched as her hands flailed vainly warding off the thieves. Pain shot through her as coldly as a snake's hiss. Blinded by tears, the baby's wail echoed in her veins.

A warm hand and gentle voice rocked her awake. 'Zessi, you were having a bad dream.'

'They stole my baby . . . they stole my baby.'

The nun's tone hardened. Her New York accent thickened. 'No, you gave the child up for adoption eight months ago. Your body grew a life of which you will have no part.'

Zessi's voice as brittle as the nun's starched habit. 'And you still won't tell me if it was a boy or girl.'

'That's correct. For the umpteenth time, it had ten fingers, ten toes, a good set of lungs and overall, very healthy.' She put Zessi's small suitcase onto the bed. 'You have healed internally and your stay has come to an end. Unless of course you want to sacrifice that diamond studded into your belly button?'

Zessi drew the nightgown close. 'Hell of a way to wake up, thanks. You're as warm as a dingo's breakfast.'

'A what?'

'A dingo. Australia's version of a wild dog.'

'And it's breakfast?'

'A piss and look around.' Zessi didn't flinch at the look of utter disdain that spread across the woman's face. Instead, jutted out her chin, and said, 'Leave me please, I need to get inside my own head without your assistance.'

Zessi waited several minutes after the door closed behind the meddlesome woman, then flung back the sheets. Her eyes traced the hideous scar of guilt, circumstances of an elaborate one-night-stand. Yet, it wasn't a small diamond that filled her belly button. As hard as she tried to deny the transaction, the settlement figure was still a good deal. Cash and jewellery. But the loss was a void that would take a long time to fill. If ever. A tragic secret. One which Zessi hoped she would take to her grave.

By lunchtime, she was back at her usual buskers' spot in Central Park reciting poetry, and nodding her gratitude to the kind folk tossing coins into her floppy hat. The much older couple who entertained passersby with their flute and violin duet, encouraged her to have lunch with them. The man, known for successfully communicating with hand motions, the woman with her trilly voice.

'We've missed you, our little vegemite!' she sang.

For the first time in a long time, Zessi hugged another human being. 'Tis folk like you, who wash away the blues. My honour to sit with you a while, for you are the reason I smile.'

The man applauded loudly, then, with both hands outwards, palms facing Zessi, he touched his thumbs and forefingers then drew them apart like a theatre curtain.

'Charades? Okay, I'll play,' Zessi grinned.

He then performed a kangaroo hop.

'An Aussie on stage?'

The woman laughed. 'Yes! She's about your age, kicking up a storm telling jokes before leading a cabaret theatre troupe.'

Suppressing the hopeful excitement, Zessi spent the rest of the afternoon accompanying the musicians and reciting Henry Lawson's Bush Poetry. By nightfall, she couldn't bear the suspense for a moment longer, and went in search of this Aussie girl on stage in Broadway.

# 1989

## Aussies In Broadway

Devastated, her thespian spark had begun to dull. Was it the dreaded decade vex? The child superstar burned out? The repetitive lines? The accents? Marnie began to fear the stage. At 23 years old, it wasn't her figure or features that had declined, but her mind. Every now and then, it would short circuit and she would forget her lines. Added to that, she hadn't heard from her family and tonight was the black-tie finale of the extremely popular stage show at Gershwin Theatre. She hoped nobody had died. Jarrod had assured her the only time he wouldn't show for a special occasion of hers was if somebody died.

Through elephant tears, she moaned, 'Why is it I can remember something said when I were a kid, and not from a ruddy show I've been doing all month . . . that I wrote?'

'Smile for the camera!' Zessi burst into the dressing room, then raced over to Marnie holding her head in her hands, shoulders heaving alongside heart wrenching sobs. 'What is it, my beautiful friend? What is it?'

'Oh Zessi. I don't want to do this anymore. Not on stage. No more. I'm tired. I wouldn't be the first to run and hide.' Marnie wailed.

'Come now, you're the star of the show! You're on the road to fame. You can't stop now! Besides, the journos love ya, luv!' Fortunately, Zessi's Aussie accent didn't let her down.

Marnie lifted her head. Through a bottom-lip wobble, said. 'Ya wag!'

Zessi gripped her best friend's shoulders and stood her up. 'One more show! Then we have a rest before our next adventure. What's gotten into you anyway?'

'Tell me how you found me. Please, Zessi?'

'Miss Marnie! You've heard that a thousand times. You know how!'

'And you know it always peps me up to hear it.'

'Fine. A short version. You need to be made-up for the dress rehearsal.' Zessi spoke quickly. 'We lost touch after junior school in Sydney. Years later, tired and hungry from busking in Central Park I walked into a cabaret and took a corner booth. There you were in your element telling your joke about the queen's wave! My heroine. The school girl who got away with not washing up after the biggest volunteer event in outer Sydney!' The women shared a giggle. 'And the rest, they say, is history.'

Marnie slumped. Pouted. 'I haven't heard from my family.'

'And that's not unusual. But there's something else flickering those flames burning in your eyes. Talk.'

'It's my memory. I don't remember what happened after that event. It's like my brain has buried something. Plus, you're also aware of how many re-takes we've been having to do. Cecil, our illustrious leader even offered tablets and powder!'

'Did you accept?'

'Oh, no. A warm lavender-scented bath in a claw foot tub will suit me just fine!'

'Yes, we all know that. And if you hopped into one after every occasion, you'd cause a sensation. Mind you, not one that Cecil would approve of . . . although your fanbase would love to get a glimpse of your Aussie arse beforehand.' Zessi slapped it for good measure.

'I'm surprised you haven't sneaked a photo with that bulky camera of yours already!'

Zessi's mischievous wink just as a solid rap on the door stopped Marnie's reply from continuing. Instead, both women swooned.

Standing ahead of the make-up artist and hairdresser, a man wearing a green fez sedating a mane of dark waves. His chiselled face as gold as the golden beaches at Cape Cod. The actress drank in his kind eyes, bent nose and blushed when her eyes settled on his mouth.

'Allo, I am Valentino. I have been appointed as your psychologist. I would rather become your friend and entice the memory inside your beautiful head to behave.'

'Oh?' Marnie said and let herself be positioned in front of the mirror by a woman wielding a hairdryer.

The party of artists prevented her from looking at the rest of Valentino's physique. All she could see was his face.

'I have a telephone call, Miss Marnie,' Zessi said amid the building racket. 'I'll be back to help you dress.'

It was the fastest get-ready act the artists performed, leaving the sizzling atmosphere safely contained in the dressing room.

'You are exquisite with and without all this plaster on your face,' Valentino said. 'I was recommended by your brother. . .'

Marnie gasped. 'Jarrod?'

'The one and only! We met by accident at a fencing convention in Amsterdam about 12 months ago. My friend had suffered an epileptic fit soon after his event. Because I specialise in training the mind, I ended up with two patients. Your brother blamed himself, and my friend needed to regain his confidence.'

'Why did Jarrod blame himself?'

'The two were competing fiercely, reputed to only stop when their bodies called the shots. That there challenged my training more than any other. It's been solid rehabilitation for months on end. Jarrod's gone back to the land of kangaroos. My friend is trying a different discipline and staying in Italy. That's my home. Venice actually.'

'Venice? Oh, such a beautiful place. But how did Jarrod know I was having problems?'

'He didn't. He doesn't. He just said you needed someone in your life who he could trust.'

Marnie rolled her eyes affectionately. 'Always looking after me! Do you know if he's going to be attending tonight's swansong?'

'Let's talk about us instead.'

'Us?'

Valentino nuzzled his chin over her shoulder. 'Yes. Do you believe in love at first sight, Marnie?'

She shrugged the opposite creamy shoulder out of her dressing gown. 'Love? I wouldn't know. Lust? Absolutely. Experienced? Not at all!'

'We wait until after the show. But first, let me read your lines to you. Concentrate on my voice. Let it and your lines etch themselves into your memory. Open your mind, flutter those beautiful eyes shut and close your sensational mouth.'

'Good luck if you think you can hypnotise me, Valentino!'

'Good luck if you think you can stop me, Marnie!'

Her laugh erupted like an unstable volcano. 'Be quick then, Zessi will be back soon.'

By the time Marnie recited her last line in unison with Valentino, Zessi had finished dressing the star of the show.

She golf-clapped her friend. 'You look and sound amazing, Miss Marnie! And I have some great news. We'll have three more Aussies in the front row tonight!'

Marnie squealed delightedly. 'My two lucky charms who have fire-bombed my dressing room with fairy dust! Let's hang out together forever!'

'I'm in!' Valentino bowed regally.

'Me too! But not all the time,' said Zessi, rather embarrassed.

'Oh! This is wonderful. Will you help me create a play?' Marnie clutched their hands.

Zessi froze, wide eyed. 'Will it be about a copper hair pin?'

'What else?'

The star of the show swept out of her dressing room, personal fans in tow. 'I must get on stage. I've got some lines to rehearse!'

'That's music to my ears,' Valentino gushed.

Zessi held back the wing's curtain. 'Always my heroine, Miss Marnie!'

# 1995

# Brooklyn, The City Of Breaking Hearts

Lights flickered and flashed. Pungent fumes raked at her airways. Her head wouldn't move. A mask descended . . . closer . . . closer . . . the little girl cried out . . .

'Wake up, Miss Marnie,' Zessi called out softly as she closed the door. 'Time to get ready.'

Eyes squeezed to extinguish the hazy dream-thread; Marnie focussed on the framed poster hanging on her makeshift dressing room door. Her very own poster design for her debuting playwright. 'The Mystical Hand Forged Copper Hair Pin'. With the latest theatrical performance feasted on by the international paparazzi, Marnie had worked it to her advantage. Declared as a fund-raising event for the homeless of Brooklyn; loyal dramatists dedicated themselves to her continued success. Media parasites provided free international advertising. Zessi shadowed her every move and Valentino, who was permanently attached to her side, another drawcard for the image-thirsty camera sharks.

'Miss Marnie, there are so many people out there. Soon they'll be climbing the trees!' Zessi chuckled as she peered out the little window.

Valentino entered and gathered up his beloved. 'Rise and shine, our star! This is going to be bigger than the Ben-Hur epic, Mar. Your family will be so proud of you.'

'Something happened . . .'

*'Good afternoon everyone, this is your Half Hour Call. Half Hour Call please. Half Hour. Thank you.'*

The love birds pulled apart as the make-up artists bustled inwards.

***

Entourage in tow with Valentino bring up the rear, Marnie paused to smile, or pose dramatically into the flashbulbs, ignoring the demanding questions.

'What's your favourite line, Miss Marnie?'

'Why the homeless? Is this something you did in Australia?'

Showing her hand in its mimicked royal wave, her popular trademark evoked the laughter she hoped. It's rippling effect swept her on stage. Her heart sank. Centre, first row, three empty seats. Teasing the crowd, she swished her oversized costume and ran from the stage, straight into Zessi's waiting arms.

'They're not here! My family aren't here. When Jarrod and I were kids, we always said . . .'

'Stop calling wolf,' she said sternly.

'I don't mean to . . .'

'Good. You have a lot of people demanding your attention. They love ya, luv!'

Marnie gulped, extended her neck and waited for Valentino and Zessi to kiss each cheek concurrently.

'We love ya, luv!' they called out after her.

The audience roared their appreciation, then gradually quietened when Marnie lit the candle.

Backstage, Valentino pulled Zessi aside. 'She'll never forgive herself if something happened.'

'Yeah. Over to you, mindbender. Any ideas?'

'Indeed, I do. I am going to propose to her after the show. We've talked about moving to Venice in the near future and she's insisted you join us. I have a villa for us and a luxury suite I know you will simply love.'

'I accept! I adore my best friend and you've grown on me like a zit.' They grinned and shook hands. 'Do you have any idea how we keep her involved in theatre without actually being on stage?'

'It won't take long for her to be recognised as a playwright.'

'We can only hope!'

'After the curtain goes up and *amore mio* is preoccupied, I'm going across to the Financial District to collect a certain piece of jewellery. Keep her busy between Acts. I'll be back before the encore.'

Zessi winked, then turned back to watch the drama on stage. With hope, her eyes traced the front row. Heart flip-flopped. Jarrod sat comfortably with an empty seat either side. His face, unreadable. Zessi smiled and joined in the resounding applause as the curtain fell.

Props changed, backdrops repositioned, the smoke machine ready to billow smoke, something made Zessi look over Marnie's shoulder as she smudged the star's make-up and tousled her hair. She smiled shyly at the approaching man.

'Miss Marnie, you have a visitor!'

'Jarrod!' she pirouetted and threw her arms out. 'Where's Mum and Dad? Are they...?'

'They've each had a heart attack. Rather embarrassing if you ask me.'

*'Five Minute Call. Five Minute Call please.'*

'Hurry up and tell us, Jarrod, I'm about to go back on stage and you need to take your seat before the curtain's go up.'

'Marnie, they were having sex! Can you believe it? At their age?' He couldn't contain his laugh. 'Sorry, but can you believe it?'

'Awkward! But Jarrod, are they okay? Can they talk? Where are they?'

He squeezed his sister's shoulder affectionately. 'Yes, they've been stabilised and insisted on getting medically transferred to San Francisco, then we're going home. I'll make sure they have the best treatment, little sister. See you at your next special occasion.'

'Do you know what they did to me?' Marnie said impulsively.

Astonished, Jarrod simply said, 'Phone home sometime,' then walked away.

*'One Minute Call. One Minute Call please. Hush.'*

Stunned, Zessi and Marnie stared at each other until the applause registered.

'Go, Miss Marnie. They love ya, luv!'

***

Marnie couldn't wait any longer. One minute to midnight, with each tick of the second hand on the wall clock she chanted, 'With a calmness paradoxical to the situation. With a calmness paradoxical to the situation.'

Time's up! She reached for the telephone. Watched the dial spin. A calm voice told her to speak.

'This is Miss Marnie. I want to report a missing person.'

'Miss Marnie! We only saw you today! Great show. But who? Who is missing?'

'My Valentino . . .'

Zessi caught the handpiece. 'This is Zessi, he left during Act One. He was going to a jewellery shop in the Financial District. It's not like him to miss the encores. Miss Marnie fears the worst.'

'Thank you. We'll send someone around when we know more.'

Standing up, Marnie hugged herself in her dressing gown. 'A jewellery shop?' she said, eyes glazed.

'Yes. He was going to propose, take you to Venice, and I was coming with you,' Zessi replied and caught her best friend.

Rocked by the rawness of it all, Marnie wailed. 'Why oh why does life keep my emotions on this horrid trampoline? Why?'

'Shhh, try and sleep, Miss Marnie.'

'I don't want to.'

'Please, luv, the shock hasn't hit you yet,' and handed her a neat whiskey.

Ten past five o'clock in the morning, the intercom chimed. Zessi whispered another prayer as she pressed the button.

'Yes?' she said.

'It's the police, we need to come up.'

'The kettle's on.'

'Good.'

Robotically, Marnie tucked herself into the classic chaise lounge. Hands nursed a strong sweet tea, and dissolving sedative. Two unfamiliar men sat opposite the women. Their hats in hand.

Sergeant Tolly and Detective Ramos introduced themselves respectively, and commended Marnie on a successful show. The men conferred silently.

Marnie's teacup chinked the saucer impatiently. 'Where is he? I know something awful has happened. I can feel it. You being here confirms it, so please, don't torture me any longer.'

Sergeant Tolly spoke solemnly. 'Miss Marnie, regrettably, we have found your Valentino. It's not easy to tell you the circumstances, so please, prepare yourselves for bad news.'

Zessi squished herself up against Marnie, placed her teacup and saucer onto the table, took her hands, and said, 'We are.'

'We're sorry to tell you that a call came in about a body hanging from the Brooklyn Bridge. It took several hours to retrieve it and have appealed for a media ban, given his relationship to you. Our condolences, Miss Marnie, Zessi.' He slid an eye-closed facial portrait onto the table.

Several minutes passed. Marnie leant forwards, murmured, 'He looks as peaceful as when he's asleep. My beloved, Valentino,' gulped twice, sniffled and said, 'What happens now?'

The officers took it in turn to explain the arduous process ahead in order to determine the cause of death, an investigation into it and depending on the coroner's report, how long it would take to have his body interred.

Sergeant Tolly cleared his throat. 'This is never an easy question to ask, but are you aware of any last wishes? Uh . . . we ask this so we know what his interment should be. It helps with the grieving process, Miss Marnie.'

She squeezed Zessi's hands. Her bottom lip trembled. 'Valentino always talked about donating his organs to save a life. If that weren't possible, being useful in medical science. He was fascinated with how the mind and body worked. But he was meant to be old when all that happened. We were meant to be old.'

Little by little, her resolve crumbled like a wet sand dune.

'Perhaps consider keeping a low profile for a while . . . just in case this was a targeted attack. We can't have our adopted superstar in any danger!' Detective Ramos smiled sadly. 'If you're going to leave town, please ensure we have your new contact details. We'll take our leave now. Again, our condolences. We'll be in touch when we know more. Take care, ladies.'

By the time Zessi returned from showing the men out, Marnie had flaked out on the lounge. After making her best friend comfortable, she reached for the telephone directory and started phoning the hospitals.

Twenty blurred days and long nights followed. The women had bickered, cried, bickered and cried some more. But tonight, Zessi had had enough and insisted on a midnight hot-toddy.

'Miss Marnie,' she ventured calmly, 'There are two things that concern me greatly. One, we haven't heard from the police and two, why would your family be travelling under a different surname?'

'What on earth do you mean?'

'With a little help, I eventually found out that they flew home, eight days ago, under the surname Kobelet.'

Marnie skulled the shot and spoke with similar vehemence. 'Eight? Eight?' Storming over to the phone, she stretched the curly cord straight. The minute her call answered she barked down the phone.

'Jarrod? Do you care to tell me what's going on?'

'Hey, little sister. Our folks are recovering steadily. So sorry to read of your sad news, really sorry.'

'Is that it?'

'You haven't been here to fully comprehend the utter complexity of the situation, Marnie. I cannot be in two places at once. I have to look after Mum and Dad.'

'But you just left! You never phoned or anything. And . . . and why the different surname?'

'For our safety, really.'

'Your safety?'

'Well? What have the police told you?'

'Nothing yet.'

'Perhaps you ought to take your frustration out on them, instead of your older brother? Hmm? Besides, it's way past your bedtime.'

'Oh Jarrod, Jarrod, I'm sorry. It's just so awful. We both feel so alone.'

'Enough of the drama, Marnie. I'm going to love and leave you. I have two bedridden parents to keep alive until you get home.'

'Is that what you want me to do?'

'Not really. Keep making it big overseas, Mum and Dad have around the clock care and very capable staff, so don't worry about any of that. Call again sometime, it's easier that way. Bye, got to run.'

Marnie stuttered and stared at Zessi. 'He hung up!'

'It's late, Miss Marnie, let's get some sleep. In the morning, I think we should phone the cops and ask questions.'

'Or just fly to Venice.'

'Let's do both.'

Marnie allowed herself to be ushered into the bedroom. To Zessi's relief, her best friend was asleep by the time her head hit the pillow.

***

Croissant crumbs, spilt espressos and a toppled vase of flowers sat upon the breakfast tray. The police had never heard of a Detective Ramos or a Sergeant Tolly. Nor had they any information on Valentino's death, or the whereabouts of his body.

# 2001
# Jalekem

Jarrod rolled up the maps at the sound of his parents slowly wheeling themselves towards the grand dining room. Time stood still. A rare luxury of being in their company. Their wispy white hair reminded him of snowflakes, and of their holiday together exploring Scandinavia in the early 1990s. His favourite aspect had been Stockholm's independent communes. The inspiration to the kingdom he was going to establish. At home. On his land. Not solely modern living. Medieval living with a few modern utilities. Jarrod detested the class definitions, and turned his nose up at the category of lower class. How degrading. His kingdom would be developed by distinctions thus determined by skillset. With his hand-selected bakers, bankers, blacksmiths, breeders, brewers, butchers, candlestick makers and husbandry specialists working alongside the other hands-on community members, typically archers, builders, guards, medical practitioners, musicians, pharmacists, scientists, and tutors. Jarrod would be the holder of the court. He would manage the treasury. Yet, he needed to declare a name of ownership to the Land. Kingdom was only ever used within its boundaries. A slow smile crept across his face. Yes! Jarrod, the Lord of . . .

'You look quite satisfied,' Leanna dabbed at her drooping lip.

'I am!' Jarrod said. 'Father, you've mixed up your buttons again. Do you do this to tease me?'

It took quite a while before Kevan formulated his words. 'Yes . . . because it is the . . . only time you spend . . . time with me.'

'I'm a busy man, Father. You mightn't remember what that was like when I was younger when your work took you away for ages at a time. Nowadays, you and Mum hang together all the time so you're definitely not lonely.' He chucked the aging cheeks playfully.

Their familiar conversation interrupted by the jangling telephone. Striding over to the French handpiece, Jarrod raised it to his ear, then remembered he could have as easily used the mobile phone. Still a foreign implement to press up against his ear, he missed half the conversation by holding it away from his ear when speaking into it. He much preferred the Alexander Graham Bell invention.

Listening intently, his shoulders sagged progressively, until he slid down the wall and sat on the floor. It took a long while before he remembered he had company.

'Pardon me, that was some disturbing news,' Jarrod said, composing himself rapidly. 'Come, come, let's have pre-dinner drinks.'

Ringing the crystal bell, Barnard (the third), soon tottered in, balancing a tray holding a carafe of mead, a silver goblet, two decorative copper cups with several little vials of tablets alongside.

'Not drinks. Medication more like it,' Leanna grizzled.

'I'm trying to keep you two lovebirds alive as long as I can. After your uncannily synchronised strokes, you need these tablets for the rest of your lives. Honestly! Playing hanky-panky in your sixties should be illegal,' Jarrod scoffed gently.

'You have no idea . . . about love. Still single. Rich and lonely.'

'Never lonely, Dad!'

'Enough, you two,' Leanna chipped. 'Who was on the telephone?'

'Zessi. Marnie's theatre has burnt to the ground. Thankfully she isn't hurt, but is in hospital under heavy sedation. So sad for her.' Jarrod said quietly. 'I don't have any further information, so there is nothing more to discuss. Let's give thanks for the food we're about to eat and count our blessings. But first, I'll straighten up your buttons, Dad.'

***

Months later while Jarrod entertained special guests; tucked away in their private suite, Kevan and Leanna worked as a team to dial Marnie's number. It took a long time. They repeatedly reached the second last digit then remembered they hadn't dialled the country code for Italy, or they remembered the country code and forgot the number for Venice. Eventually, they got the sequence correct and squeezed each other's hands to the ringing pulse.

'*Buongiorno*? Hello?' Marnie's voice echoed down the line.

'Marnie!'

'Mum? Dad?'

The three parties talked over the top of each other.

'Stop!' Marnie yelled. 'Where are you?'

'In our suite,' Kevan said.

Thank God they're not using the mobile, Marnie thought. 'Okay, find the little button that has a speaker on it . . . like a loudhailer picture. Press it.'

After several games of telephone tag, they finally managed to have a conversation.

'Sorry to hear about . . . fire.

'Thanks Dad, yes, it was all terribly sad. Zessi's been my guardian angel. She always has. I've picked up the pieces and with everlasting thanks to my beloved Valentino, I was accepted into the Venetian culture years ago. Has Jarrod been looking after you two?'

'Yes. Dad and I want you to come home.'

'Not yet, Mum. Valentino bequeathed me a rather gorgeous studio with the most perfect terrace overlooking St. Mark's Square. After the theatre disaster, Zessi finally convinced me to move in permanently.'

'Glad sh . . . she's there,' Kevan said.

'So am I, Dad! What's news?'

'Jarrod work hard. He built a pri . . . private museum with plans . . . for a bigger kitchen. Mum sews. I get words wrong on puzzles. Very tiring.'

'Has my suite changed? And the attic? Have you been in there?'

'Yes. You have the top storey. Attic locked. No . . . not since you were a little girl.'

'Your father is tiring, Marnie. I might drool, but at least I can hold a conversation. After our untimely medical incidents, Jarrod insisted we retain our independence until we can't control our faculties. Such a considerate man. So, we happily stay on our storey, have access to the balcony and everything we need. The staff are wonderful, we just need to ring the bell or press the intercom button. Jarrod's doing very well with his career.' Leanna slurped, pardoned herself, then took a deep breath. 'Marnie, what will you do now? Have you got your own affairs in order? Have you got any work lined up? Do you need money? You should come home.'

Marnie had anticipated the inquisition and added more lavender into the slowly filling bathtub.

'Mum, I'm a grown woman, so yes, by now I have got my affairs in order! Granted I've suffered some tragedies, had some terrific successes and now happily settled into Venetian life. I am reworking a play I started years ago. The artisans here love me, my work and are very supportive. I have been promised an audience at the Sforza Castle in Milan for a gala event they're planning. Isn't that so exciting?'

Annoyingly, static broke through the line.

'Hello? Mum? Dad? You still there?'

'Yes, Marnie. The line went funny but you said something about a castle. Will we be invited? Your father and I haven't seen a castle since Jarrod took us through Scandinavia.'

Marnie grumped. 'We were talking about me. I've flown you and Dad, and Jarrod for that matter, to places where you've all borne witness to my special occasions and experienced the richness in history. I am just as successful as Jarrod is.'

'When are you going to stop acting, and start living in the real world? And while we're on that subject, please tell me you have retired that fable?'

'That fable? It went up in smoke.' Marnie sobbed against the back of her hand. Having an argument was the last thing she had in mind. Her retort was stronger than she intended. 'I don't act! I live. I create characters and make them real. Besides, the fable as you coldly refer to it, has driven me my whole life. And, for the record, it will be my swansong. I intend to announce my retirement after my performance in Milan.'

'Nevertheless, Marnie, we won't be alive forever. You need to come home. There are some things that will not be spoken about over a blasted telephone.'

'I want to speak to Dad.'

'He's asleep. Incidentally, have you heard of genomes and Cryonics?'

'Of course I have! They're the latest topics of conversation at dinner parties. Where do you think I live, Mum? Under a rock?'

'Well, when the time comes, we want to be cremated. Remind Jarrod of that. Right now, I'm exhausted and we have to take a series of medication before we retire. We send our love and best wishes. Come home, Marnie.'

'Mum, wait a moment please. In 1995, you all flew home under a different surname. Why?'

'Can't recall that. You'll have to ask Jarrod.'

'Okay, let's try this one. Where is the journal and things the old man left for me?'

'For you? Heavens, you are in your own spotlight! Come home, Marnie.'

Flabbergasted at having the line disconnected without a warm word, Marnie ran herself a bath. While she waited, poured herself a long hot-toddy.

***

In the darkest hour of the following morning; Jarrod was still rattled. He groomed then galloped his favourite mare over the mini steeple chase. Charged her through the jousting lanes. Drenched in perspiration, he led her into the moat. While she cooled, he swam as hard as his aging body would allow. In perfect timing to an ominous burnt orange sunrise, the wing song of a lone magnificent white swan tamed Jarrod's ire. Back at the stables, he did the grooming.

Unaccustomed to silence in the house, he grew rather concerned when his parents hadn't emerged. Instead of taking the elevator, scaled the stairs two at a time and rapped loudly on their door. Several times. Eventually, Mother greeted him. She was perfectly attired. As was his father, surprisingly. There was a distinct coolness in the air.

'Morning Mum, Dad. You had me concerned.'

'We had hoped you would come looking for us,' Leanna said calmly. 'Father, you have something to say?'

'Ye. . . yes, morning Son. Won't you . . . join us for break. . . breakfast?'

Jarrod baulked. This wasn't his dining room. This didn't feel right. Soon after the jingling bell, their usual butler wheeled in a trolley laden with gleaming plate domes. Jarrod could taste the buttery, flaky croissants before he even smelt them.

'Why not! I am actually quite ravenous.' He dutifully waited until his parents were settled, then took his seat.

'You look a tad frazzled, everything okay?'

'Actually no, Mum. I feel like I was ambushed via telephone by my dear little sister. You really stirred things up talking about cremations and cryonics! Really? You know how dramatic she can be!'

Kevan leant forwards. 'Cremate me. I want to trans . . . trans . . . transition!' His determination evident with the fist pump.

'We will not discuss that topic at breakfast.' Leanna stated. 'How do you think Marnie is . . . you know, in the head?'

'Why?'

'Oh, we had a bit of a heated conversation last night, that's all.'

'You did,' Kevan pointed at his wife, 'not me. We must . . . speak again to her . . . soon. I must.'

Leanna practically force-fed him a croissant. 'Hush up.'

Jarrod grimaced at his mother's recollection of the telephone call. He countered Marnie's ire with ongoing grief, loneliness and rapid retirement. A silence settled over the table as thick as the freshly squeezed orange juice being poured from the crystal decanter. Old Barnard (the third) resumed serving breakfast, then shuffled out of the room.

'And now she's talking about some gala event at a castle in Milan!' Leanna continued.

'Yes, Marnie mentioned that. There's other things she mentioned, well, questioned, actually.'

'What . . . about?'

'She discovered we flew out under a different surname.'

'What did you say?'

'Not much. The more pressing matter though. . . let's go way back to the night you returned from the soup kitchen. She wants to know what happened because she cannot account for several of her teenage years. Care to share, Mum?'

Leanna huffed. 'Marnie is well aware some conversations must be held in person. If you want to be useful in that department, entice our drama queen to travel back with us after Milan.'

Jarrod looked at his father fumbling for his handkerchief. His eyes darted from side to side, conveying a type's warning which shook Jarrod to the core. Instinct demanded he didn't continue with the subject.

'Well, I'm not about to ruin breakfast!' he muttered and tucked in heartily.

In between mouthfuls, exuberantly revealed great news.

'I hereby announce my very own kingdom, of which you are very much a part of.'

'Kingdom?' An endearing, toothy grin appeared on Kevan's face.

'Yes, Dad. I will be the Lord.'

'The Lord. . . too?' he guffawed, totally startling his wife.

Her shrill outburst almost shattering the chandelier above their heads. 'The Lord? Of what?'

'Of where? That ought to be your question, Mum. Of where?'

Exasperated, she said, 'Of where, then?'

'Jalekem.'

'Of where?' Leanna spluttered.

'Jalekem,' Jarrod announced proudly. 'The first two initials of all our names, except . . .'

'Marnie's,' Kevan muttered. 'Not Marnie's.'

'Bravo, Dad! No, it just didn't sound right. She'll get over it. It's not her kingdom. She owns this historical building.'

'Will you have a flag?' Leanna asked quietly.

'Oh! Great suggestion.'

'Crest. You . . . must have . . . a crest.'

The discreet ringing mobile phone in his pocket was the timely interruption Jarrod desperately sought. Brushing crumbs from his mouth, he excused himself.

Out of ear shot, said, 'Hope you're in a better mood. Have you got a date?'

'Yes, and yes,' Marnie said. 'August 28, 2002.'

'Perfect! That'll time in nicely with the conclusion of the medieval event being held in the Netherlands.'

'Excellent. As usual, Zessi is in charge of the travel arrangements. Does that still work for you?'

'Absolutely. I have an assistant now too, aside from Old Barnard. It's Damon.'

Marnie gasped. 'Our Old Barnard? Surely not!'

'No, this is Barnard the third! That's not his real name, but he's happy to continue with tradition!'

'And Damon? Your mate from school?'

'Yeah! He's a splendid scientist.'

'Really? Why would a medieval historian need a scientist?'

'Why do you act?' Jarrod countered.

'Hmm. Fine. What name will you be travelling under this time?'

'I missed that, say again.'

'Did Mum or Dad have any answers for you?'

'Bad connection. Chat when we do, my dear little sister.' Jarrod disconnected the call and went looking for Damon.

# 2002
# Death in Turin

'Have you heard from Zessi?' Marnie paced laps around her dressing room. Knuckles white from clutching the cell phone. 'She's not answering her phone.'

'I'm sure she's on her way,' Jarrod's voice, muffled by the racket of a busy terminus in the background. 'How do you think we feel? We're waiting to pull out of Turin Station. Been sitting on this blasted train for ages. For a relatively short journey from Paris, it certainly feels extraordinarily long.'

'I can imagine. But this is the first time in an awfully long time that Zessi hasn't been here to do up my dress!'

Blissfully, the background noises subsided.

'Is that all you're worried about, Marnie?'

'Mum! No, that's definitely not all I'm worried about. I love Zessi. She's been my everything since we reconnected back in the 80s! Worse still, you're all going to be late for my special occasion!' Marnie stepped onto her balcony. 'Oh, how I so wish you and Dad could see the magnificent fountains and courtyards! Absolutely exquisite. Even though the city in August is blissfully quiet with the locals hitting the beach, a lot are actually attending tonight!'

'I'm sure they are, dear, I'm sure they are. We'll be there as quickly as we can. Even if it is for the encore! While we're waiting, I can tell you that we had a marvellous time at the medieval event. Just marvellous. Your father enjoyed the mead and jousting. Amsterdam in general, actually! He's very tired and blows you a kiss. Jarrod's swordsmanship and craft awarded him an audience with the . . .'

'Hello?' Marnie glared at the annoying piece of technology. 'No signal. Ugh, so annoying.'

Her make-up and dressing team bustled into her room. 'We can't wait any longer, Miss Marnie, the guests are getting extremely restless.'

Eventually, dutifully obliging her hosts, Marnie put on a brave face and swept onto the stage. Her treasured emerald green velvet wing-back chair, her only comfort. Marnie sat. She got lost in time. She looked for the old man.

A jingle in the wings roused her from her reverie. 'Ladies and gentlemen, I am going to recite my absolute favourite story written a very, very long time ago by A Non. It isn't a long story, but it does raise a lot of questions. The author's name is top of my list.' She paused dramatically. 'Hmm, anonymous or a non de plume?

Silence befell her enthralled audience.

***

Meanwhile, back in Turin, the train conductor's voice announcing an extended delay caused an uproar from its passengers. Eventually, under a strong police presence, they were encouraged to disembark for their own comfort. An entire section of the platform was cordoned off leaving a narrow walkway into the terminus.

Once settled, Jarrod left his parents nursing very strong coffees. He approached a young policeman who had just encouraged a journalist from getting too near the blockade.

'Can you speak English?' Jarrod said.

'Oui. Yes.'

'Good. It's obviously not a broken-down train holding us up, constable, what's actually going on?' Jarrod asked.

'I am not able to say.'

'Who can, then? I'm late for a very important function at the Sforza Castle.'

The policeman studied Jarrod, then gasped. 'You're Miss Marnie's famous brother! Oh, monsieur, pardon.' He stepped in closer and lowered his voice. 'Someone played chicken with the train and lost. Travel by rail to Milan will be cancelled until forensics have arrived, then the remains have to be removed. Impossible to identify the victim, sadly.'

Jarrod paled, nodded his thanks and turned away. For the first time in years, he bummed a cigarette. With fingers crossed, left a message on Marnie's mobile.

'My dear little sister, we will be unable to attend tonight's performance therefore shall be returning to Sydney, pronto.'

***

Alone on a chilly Christmas Eve, Marnie nursed a sherry and rubbed her ear. She tried in vain to force the squeals of happy children out of her memory, yet it had been lovely to hear mother's joy describing her father's gig at playing Santa. Marnie had pressed the telephone to her ear so hard when he stuttered his way through his message for her, it still ached. Now, she waited ever so patiently for her brother to return her call.

Years since the Brooklyn incident and months since the travesty which claimed some poor person's life, Marnie still couldn't believe it had been Zessi. Yet, in the same notion, couldn't comprehend why her best friend would have just disappeared. The anger at being jilted and a rousing suspicion that she had been lied to by her family long-since subsided, it seemed fitting to become a recluse after her retirement.

Mesmerised by the misted festive lights swaying lazily to faint strains of carollers braving the bleak Venice weather, Marnie almost jumped out of her skin when the telephone rang. Jarrod's tipsy voice shouting with revellers in the background wasn't pleasant at all. What she could deduce was: *she wasn't to ask questions over the telephone, her parents were doing well with their recovery and there was no need for her to hurry home.* Each time Marnie went to speak, a folly of horns interrupted. When the call dropped out, she sent Jarrod a text.

*Sounds like you're at a fox hunt!*

His prompt reply, surprising. *We are. Enjoy retirement. Ciao bella.*

Marnie screwed up her nose and muttered, 'Ciao bella? How unusual.'

Soon, elephant tears trickled down her cheeks. The lingering questions of Valentino and Zessi stabbed her as deeply as the scent of lavender filled her boudoir.

When threads of sleep finally wove their magic, Marnie dreamt of her mother's porcelain doll holding the Twisted Goblet, with Ox Cart

Annie's diamond studded painted fingernail erect like a straw. Words smeared on a crushed velvet journal levitated, then splattered across a vibrating stage curtain. It burst open and a child's voice chanted, *touch the mannequin*. As the volume increased, so did the billowed drapes. Marnie fought back the fabric as it reached for her. Eventually, it did.

She screamed herself awake when something fluttered across her cheek. Milky moonlight cut a line across her bed and up the wallpaper, illuminating the magnificent chandelier of The Malibran Theatre. Widened eyes reversed their path to the open patio doors. Marnie gasped and cocked her head.

Rowdy partygoers were singing out her name. 'Miss Marnie! Merry Christmas, Miss Marnie. We miss you, Miss Marnie.'

She couldn't resist. Wrapped herself up warmly and stepped onto her patio. The moment they saw her, they applauded. A young man stepped forwards and blew her kisses. The group started giggling nervously, then quickly hushed.

'Our theatre group cordially invite you to a private viewing of a three-act play we have written. We present it to you on New Year's Eve.'

'Where?' Marnie said.

Shyly confident, he said, 'In your drawing room! Please?'

'Come back then. No promises.' Marnie swiftly stepped out of view.

'Thank you, Miss Marnie! We love you! We miss you! Thank you! Merry Christmas.'

Their overjoyed voices, music to her ears. With her face coming to life, Marnie knew right there and then her retirement wasn't going to be as quiet as she had anticipated. As she lay back upon her pillow, the dreamscape of Ox Cart Annie's forefinger tracing its way down the handwritten pages consumed Marnie's mind. Her father's message, an echoing lullaby.

# 2034
# Homecoming

Toying with the handle of her parasol, Marnie rued her decision for not arriving a fortnight earlier. She wouldn't have changed anything to do with the Service, but using a hologram to depict the last waltz was just plain weird. Jarrod's addiction to the fandangle applications left her cold.

The garden chapel at the city's biggest church had been the sensible venue for Leanna and Kevan's memorial. Attendees consisted of offspring of the many friends of the dearly departed, dutifully paying their respects to a couple whose hearts beat as one, lived as one and died as one. At the ripe old age of 93, their love story came to an end. As did lucrative contributions to the volunteer fundraising syndicates.

With their combined ashes housed in a steel gorget—its steel collar designed to protect the neck and chest in medieval times—was a fitting vessel according to Jarrod. Even more so as he handcrafted it in his own forge. A tale of honour he talked a lot about to the gathered crowd.

Enigmatic in life as in death, their parents had set the longevity record for forgetfulness, or self-diagnosed dementia. It was a surprise for Marnie to learn that after her achievement of the acting scholarship, Leanna and Kevan had removed themselves from the public eye. Time didn't grace her to ponder on that thought. The guests regaled many a story of the wonderful volunteering events the late pair had hosted.

Whispered rumours told greater stories than the questions which begged for answers. But two questions were always the loudest. Was it Leanna or Kevan who had inherited the stately manor? And from whom? Dutifully and politely, the orphans denied all such knowledge and artfully navigated conversations away from such matters, yet entertained the bearers with snippets of their own career pre-retirement. Jarrod, a renowned historian and acclaimed blacksmith, had kept the ancient craft alive through masterclasses and by coordinating medieval reenactments around the world for almost five decades. His private collection of armouries while well regarded, wasn't open for public viewing. And Marnie, the esteemed pantomime queen with her trademark curls, had, in later years, carved out a niche for herself as a very popular playwright in Venice. The artisans claimed her as their own, loved her creativity and couldn't get enough. That's all the public knew. Marnie detested the idea of digitising her life. Very few people knew about her dear friend, Zessi, who she missed terribly. Even less people knew about Valentino's death and the mystery surrounding it. Troublesome thoughts gnawed at Marnie's mind. Again. What happened after junior school? Where was the journal? Why couldn't answers be given over the phone?

***

During the long homeward bound journey with several lily sprays beside her and the stainless vessel on her lap, Marnie peered into her reflection of the darkened windows, and recalled every momentous occasion her parents and Jarrod did manage to attend her performances. Those memories were her favourite. Highschool was a blur. Getting to the Americas, a blur. Acting scholarship? And Zessi? Their meeting a blur. Yet her absence left an ache in Marnie's heart. The frayed memory of Valentino saw fit to tease her heartstrings. Her self-absorbed guilt of trying to keep an old fable alive, ate at her very soul.

Zessi. Again. Marnie's mind was addled. But why did it always reoccur with the thought of Zessi? That recollection, combined with the recent celebration of parents' life compelled Marnie to bury her head in her hands and weep. The first real tears she had shed for a very, very long time.

The suffocating emptiness of not having a child nor spouse to pass on her legacy, threatened to implode. Marnie gripped the sterile vessel, shaking her head in disbelief. Her biggest failing was thinking she had forever to get answers to her questions. Finally admitting to herself in retirement, that her life in theatre had been a solution to hide her fears behind a veil of makeup and fakeness, had marginally lifted the darkness. A lingering memory of being a girl who clutched desperately to a blanket, clung to the corners of her mind. Concentrating on the thread, it dissolved, and suddenly she was a young woman on stage reciting 'Among School Children' by W.B. Yeats. Oh, how she related to the Irish poet and his pain of being out of touch with the modern world. She raised her head and returned Jarrod's gaze. Her question, silently asked, *do you know what happened, or not?*

***

Jarrod, greyer and further stooped, studied his little sister from the opposite side of the limousine. Their friendship had stretched with time, distance, and lack of regular communication, but, *he* had always been the one who returned home. That asset may belong to Marnie, but the improvements within, and its grounds were *his*. *He* lived in the real world. Not the make-believe. It was *he* who took on the responsibility of organising the staff to nurture their aging parents. *He* organised the building renovations to accommodate their eventual frailty. *He* paid for the extension and fortification of the old barn. *His* haven. *He* designed the science lab and museum both with its secret entrances. Gateways to *his* own second world.

The older staff shone the home's marble floors on the ground floor, beautifully reflecting the polished antique furniture and many chandeliers. The splendid rugs scattered over polished timber floors on the other storeys were kept spotlessly fresh. Their offspring manicured the lawns, hedges, horse paddocks and the trailing rose bush that now encroached the façade of the upper wing, almost completely covering the attic window. And the outline of the blasted mannequin. Jarrod's circle of trust as tight as the memory of the old man. His two personal blacksmiths provided tuition. He crafted the exemplary mead. His own community well established. New babies soon to be born for nurture and study. His Counsel, worried about those who threatened the integrity of the Land, served to persuade Jarrod to increase his army.

In time, for him, all this wouldn't matter, but Marnie's return home was essential. She still had a purpose to serve. Jarrod's decision had been made easier when her wardrobe had arrived one month prior, out of the blue.

He steepled his fingers and tentatively broached the subject of residency. 'The upper storey is yours, with your very own entrance and separate access for the staff. All by elevator and very discrete so they won't interfere with your routine. None of whom you will remember. And, of course, the attic. I battle with those stairs nowadays, Marnie.'

Her bottom lip twitched. 'Nowadays? You mean you've been up there recently?'

He scoffed. 'Not since that damned rat bore its beady eyes into my soul.'

'Oh, very dramatic, Jarrod!' Marnie said teasingly, then sobered. 'I owe you a lot of thanks. I'll begin with you being there for Mum and Dad right up to the end. You never bestowed any pressures on me to come home earlier.' The pause was so natural, it surprised them both. They smirked at the same time. 'I gladly accept. However, I suspect there was something else you need to tell me, dear brother?' Marnie said.

'Your perception should never be doubted.'

'I beg to differ. Alas, those are stories for another time. Please continue.'

Jarrod turned his head and preened his silver-sprinkled beard. 'You often came up in conversation when I sat with Mum and Dad after Brooklyn, considerably less after Turin though.'

'Guilt, do you think?'

'What? No! I believe it was their forgetfulness that had a lot to with it because often I found them simply staring at your pantomime posters.'

More tears threatened to spill down Marnie's cheeks. 'It was so long ago, I don't remember what was said, but the hurt and emotional confusion will last until my dying days. And I still don't know how I ended up in America.'

'Perhaps think about better times to carry with you into your twilight years, hmm?' Jarrod leant over and gently patted her hands. 'I'm unsure how you feel about surprises these days, but there have been a lot of changes at home. Mostly the grounds itself. Besides, there are greater things you need to know.'

Marnie reclined her seat, and said, 'Oh, I am so glad you have this model of limo! My head is aching, as are my bones. You couldn't have picked a better setting for their memorial; it's such a pity it's so far away from home!'

'To pass the time, I want you to shut your eyes, open your mind and close your mouth, my dear little sister, for I am going to tell you a story. You'll know when to speak!'

Marnie glared at him. 'Why did you send Valentino to me?'

'I liked the guy, wanted you pair to . . .' his voice trailed off and tears filled his eyes. 'Marnie, I did everything I could to make sure his death didn't end up the cold case it did. It was just all so sad. I also lost a good mate.

The tension thickened.

'I am sorry for other things too,' he added.

'Oh? Like what?'

'Back in '95. It was on advice we flew out with a different surname, particularly as the finger pointed to The Provisional IRA.'

'You tell me this now? When there's sod all anybody can do? Besides, he was Italian, not Irish!'

'Oh Marnie, we've got connections to the Irish! Hell, you really did live in dreamland.'

'Did I really have a choice?' she bristled. 'And after Turin? What advice did you receive then?'

'Medical. The drama rocked Mum and Dad to the core. Dying in a foreign country is more of a headache for the survivors than grief.'

'You seem to know about that too.'

Jarrod removed his glasses, rubbed his eyes and explained that he had accepted a role as a historian guide in the Scottish Highlands in his mid-thirties. A group of tourists had been involved in a bus crash. One of the deceased was an Australian. He could speak the language and vowed he would never be in that situation again.

'That's why I fled. We fled. I'm a coward, Marnie. Sorry.'

She let the self-pity card lay where it fell, sat back and said quietly, 'Do you believe I caused all the travesties?'

'It had crossed my mind, with the coincidences *et al*, but if it is a curse, it's one you have to live with.'

'That's a bit callous!'

'Not really. That blasted story was your obsession . . .'

'You used to read it with me!'

Jarrod smirked. '*Used to* being the operative. Can we talk about something else now?'

'Not yet. What of . . . ' Marnie squinted, desperately trying to extract the almost forgotten names. 'Ramos and . . . Tolly?'

'Have no idea.'

Tired and heavy eyed, Marnie simply said, 'You had another story to tell?'

Jarrod hummed a soothing melody, caught the eye of his driver who nodded. While drumming an accompanying rhythm on the leather armrest, Jarrod raised the soundproof screen behind Marnie. The aged features on her face softened and she sighed deeply. Jarrod murmured her name. She didn't reply.

He began his story.

'You're going to relive the enchantment of the secret room. Smell the musty fabrics. Feel the cold metal. Mum left you, me and Dad amid the thespian props and suits of armour. Much later that night, I saw her carry you to the car then drive away with Dad. At breakfast the next morning, Old Barnard the original, told me that you had had a seizure and he was to look after me until our parents came back. It was the summer holiday and I didn't care because I had the whole joint to myself. A young man. Free to do as I pleased. So, I did! I reigned my castle. I plotted how to protect our land from those who threatened to take it away. It proved to be a wise move because Mum and Dad were correct . . . people once disputed our ownership of it.'

Marnie's steady breathing and rapid eye movement indicated she was still under his spell.

'I digress. The old man who guarded the stage was our grandfather, on Mum's side and lived the life of Riley in his own childhood home. He taught me so much! Before he passed, he told me it had been the best years of his adult life. It most certainly was the most influential time of my life, yet I dedicated the rest of it to a man I barely knew. Rather odd when you think about it.'

He stared at the gorget and grinned. 'Oh, this feels so good. Anyway, Mum and Dad returned home long after he passed. By then, your career had taken off. Zessi was in your shadow and then Valentino came into your life. Two absolutely wonderful people and all thanks to me! Me! Did you hear that? *Me*!' He exhaled loudly.

'Back to our parents. They aged swiftly, never did give up any information on the past. The old man and I had already put things in place for their retirement. Their eventual semi-vegetative state was imperative for the estate's progression. Simply no other way to do it. They accepted the fluctuating cognitive tides.'

'Is that what you have planned for me?'

Jarrod stopped drumming the leather at Marnie's sudden mutter.

'No,' he replied, his tone as smooth as the timber inlay door handle.

He resumed tapping and humming, and only began speaking when Marnie's face relaxed, breath deepened.

'Mum never knew the significance of the white swans. I never told her about the old man and he never talked about the journal. Anyway, he did convince me that you would come home when you were ready. And look . . . fast forward to current day, here you are! I don't live in the house. The middle storey, including all its wings is my personal space. Ground level, as always, the place of entertainment. One section has nothing to do with you.'

Jarrod stopped drumming, lowered the soundproof screen and said, 'One, two, three. Me and Damon had a crush on Zessi.'

Marnie's eyes fluttered opened. She ran her tongue around her mouth. 'Don't be cruel. Besides we were just kids.'

He turned to look out the window. 'Fortunately for you, you slept through the suburban sprawl. Look! There's the old knoll. Remember climbing that, Marnie?'

Fuzzy-headed, she said, 'Sure do, and it means we're almost home. I hope you never moved the mannequin from the attic.'

'Hush now. There's something more important. Ever looked through a sunroof while a vehicle was moving, little sister?'

'No! But I will if you will, big brother!'

As the driver slowed the vehicle, Jarrod helped Marnie steady herself against the open roof. She whipped off her hat and let her greying curls fly free.

'Jarrod! Why are we stopping here? I can't see anything except an ugly stone wall and a. . . what on earth? A drawbridge? Is that really a drawbridge?'

Marnie couldn't believe her eyes. The massive timber construction lowered over a span of water. Two guards atop the bridge tower waved a green and white flag bearing an indeterminable crest. Another two trumpeters announced their arrival. The peals rippled across the waterway.

Craning her neck this way and that, said, 'Jarrod, why do we have a moat? The walls are so high! The grass, it's all . . .' Her voice faded away as the attic window came into view, almost covered with trailing roses, trellised into an oddly familiar shape. The setting sun, painting the western wall a burnt copper.

She gasped, clutched at her heart dramatically, and leant into her brother. 'The hair pin! No! Jarrod, it's not safe.'

'It most certainly is.'

'But you don't know everything.'

'I know enough. Hush now and listen to the Lord of Jalekem.'

Marnie looked at him as if he had fallen from another planet. 'Who of where?'

At that moment, four forest-green cloaked men on magnificent white horses pulled alongside the vehicle as it neared the main entrance of the manor. Waiting for them, a dapple-grey mare with a splendid silver mane, snorted and hoofed the ground.

'Jarrod! What have you done?'

'Exactly what was required. Welcome home. You'll be shown to your suite as you look a bit tired. Dinner will be brought to you. I shall see you on the morrow. Sleep well.'

'Like you can tell me what to do?'

'I just have. I am the Lord of Jalekem. Nobody comes or goes without my saying so. My community stay within their boundaries, in the first instance you shall do well to remember that.'

'You make it sound like I'm not going home!'

He popped a tablet into his mouth, swallowed, took a deep breath and puffed out his chest as he straightened before her very eyes. His voice sounded rougher. Foreign even. 'Ah, but you are home.'

'Help me down, please. Enough of this nonsense, Jarrod. Just because I have retired from being a drama queen, I don't expect you to replace me! Next, you'll be telling me to meet you at the Twisted Goblet at midnight!'

He gestured to a relatively older man, wearing a stormtrooper's leg armour. 'Jeeves here will be at your service. You will do well to remember your position in my Kingdom.'

'Really? And what is that?'

'Maid Marnie!' Jarrod's shrill laugh got lost in a chorus of hungry dogs beyond the hedged wall.

'Dogs too?'

'Yes. Twelve of them.' He nodded his head towards Jeeves, who assisted Marnie from the vehicle with ease.

'Ma'am, allow me to show you your residence.'

Bewildered, Marnie looked at her brother as if he were a stranger. 'Twelve? Like the Knights?'

He nodded curtly, spun around and effortlessly mounted his horse.

Astonished at the fluid moment, snapped, 'We are in the year of 2034 you foolish old man, not 1834.'

'Lord of Jalekem is home.' Erect in the saddle, eye cast over his vast Land, clicked his tongue and simply trotted away.

'I must be dreaming,' Marnie whispered under her breath.

# Down Memory Lane

Long after the silent service attendant had removed the empty plates of carpaccio, roast lamb and garden vegetables, and a delicious dessert of peaches and cream, Marnie still couldn't lose the thick, sweet taste of alcoholic honey coating her teeth. Eating dinner alone was nothing new to her. However, eating it in a controlled air-conditioned suite, was. Everything smelt and felt sanitised. She never really paid attention to this suite as a child, given it was her parents private space, but was quite perplexed there weren't any windows nor balcony overlooking their beautiful gardens behind the manor. Just one long, blank wall.

Submerged in a mountain of lavender-scented bubbles, comprehension eluded her. Wrinkling like a prune wasn't going to achieve anything, Marnie reminded herself sternly.

The stairs to the attic were steeper and more silent than she remembered. Eventually, she pushed open the heavy door. *No, no no!* An ornate chair had been positioned near the door which caught Marnie's fall. She stared into the almost bare room. Staring back at her, the mannequin. Its left hand, limp as always, but attached to the right hand, a dolly. It was her mother's! The one Marnie was never ever allowed to touch. But where was everything else? The suitcases? The forbidden trunks? Even the carpet had been removed. Marnie sniffed then realised it was the scent of roses she could smell. Dreading the weight of the aged window, she mustered all her strength, pushed outwards and ended up with a face full of blooms. Perfume combined with echoed sounds of entertainment added to her fright.

Dazed, she asked herself, 'Why am I in the attic?'

***

The town crier tolled the bell. Fanfare burst through the night air and dancers rejoiced around the campfire. Jarrod paraded with a bundle wrapped in a blanket. Once behind his lectern, silence settled, aside from the bray of the village donkey.

'Another baby has been born! That brings our population to 53. After ten years of trying, the second child and first daughter to our crier and seamstress. Granddaughter to our very own artist and great granddaughter to our original populator.' Jarrod declared. Then with a deep bow, said, 'I present you, my first queen of hearts.'

A greying stout woman, younger than Jarrod, allowed herself to be lifted out of her wheelchair. Supported by two handmaidens, she said, 'I, Zessi of Jalekem offer my congratulations. This sweet child will have fame and fortune of which she shall share. Long may you all live long into the future.'

The community whistled and hollered their delight until Zessi rotated her elevated right hand frailly.

'Once upon a time, I had a dear friend who would tell a joke about this particular wave, perhaps one day you may find yourselves a witness to the same. I'm sure her legacy has been recorded somewhere. I have had a wonderous journey, alas my time is nearly at an end.'

The engaged crowd displayed various levels of sadness and disappointment, until the donkey brayed, again. Zessi's instantaneous laugh set about a ripple of guffaws gradually increasing in volume.

She beckoned for Jarrod. 'Now the time is right. This is how the people shall remember me.'

***

After retracing her steps, Marnie stood at the doorway and surveyed the rather bare attic. 'Ah! The mannequin!' she uttered crossly.

Ever so gently, she untied her mother's porcelain dolly and laid it on the floor. Temptation got the better of her and removed the limp wrist. To her dismay, the sock was replaced by a slip of paper.

As if penned swiftly by an unfamiliar hand, two words: RUN AWAY

Shoving it deeply into her pocket, she reattached the wrist. Incentivised, with hands either side of the mannequin Marnie twisted the torso off its base. At long last she remembered all of her father's Christmas message. *'Let it end with you.'*

Atop the journal, wrapped in green felt, the hand-forged copper hairpin. Marnie cried out in dismay and shoved the lot down the front of her dress. In a trance, repositioned the mannequin, snapped off a rose, closed the window and retreated to her suite.

Hours later, she was still at a complete and utter loss as to the relevance of all the names. Between 1798 and 1855, none of the dukes, duchesses or knights meant anything at all. No clues, nor annotations in the margins or footnotes. Nothing. Pleased to read that her mother hadn't totally lied, Ox Cart Annie was actually a real person who not only owned a theatre, but also managed quite the gambling syndicate. It was simpler to deduce the wax-dobbed-nominees were children of noble families, persuaded to be runners, therefore money could easily be gotten and forgotten. Marnie nodded her head acknowledging the smart, untouchable, well disguised woman. A large tear rolled down her cheek when Ox Cart Annie's reign ended in an horrific fire in 1874. Interestingly, the woman was survived by two (known) minors. Perpendicular to the entry were two names: *Liliana and Keevin*. Underneath, in different handwriting and coloured ink: Irish second cousins?

Marnie pulled an ugly face. Hurriedly flicking through the thin pages, she noticed a dogeared corner of the year 1888. Underneath the fold, two letters: *L & K*. Scribbled in the margin was a ship's name *PS Rouen*. On the following page, a rough pencil sketch of a woman annotated as: *Mistress of Robes (Anne) dec 1895*?

There was nothing outstanding until 1941. A single entry. Unrecognisable cursive. *Leanna will attend school with Kevan. They shall get married.* Following several blank pages, Marnie burst into tears at the sight of her mother's handwriting.

*1948. Dad and I discovered mother and Aunt Annie hanging from the train bridge. Dad said they were cursed from across the Irish sea.*

Her mother's writing continued in 1952. *This blasted tale forced dad to leave just to keep me safe. Now I have to live with this blasted secret. Blasted Irish. Blasted curse. I miss my dad.*

Marnie sobbed, 'Oh my beloved Valentino, oh no. Oh my dear Zessi. I am so sorry, I never knew.'

Her breath faltered at the entry in 1961. *Son, Jarrod, healthy, old soul. Sweet child.*

During the year of Marnie's birth, 1966, an unfamiliar older person's handwriting: *Should a girl be borne, keep her safe.*

Flicking through several more blank pages, Marnie was just about to slam it closed, when another dog-eared page caught her eye. She gasped, shoved the journal and clip inside her dress, and fled as quickly as her old legs could take her down the stairs.

***

Meanwhile, calls of roosting swans drifted amid the flickering firelight dancing along the meandering waterway. Jarrod downed another two pills, waited a couple of moments then scooped up Zessi, who feebly expressed her wrath.

'Why is it that you have these youth-engineering tablets and used me as an experiment? Then my daughter . . .'

'Our daughter . . . '

'Our ovaries!'

'My sperm. You cannot design a foetus without sperm and ova. That is not rocket science, Zessi, that is creating life.'

'In the natural way . . . not in some lab, and not. . . not related.'

'Modified, if you don't mind. Besides, you and I rolled like thunder in the swankiest of penthouses at the time.' He then pecked her forehead with each word, 'Not. In. A. Lab.'

'Humph. Except, ever since, that's all you and Damon do. All the experiments, deformities, failures . . .'

'That's enough. You don't think I cried?'

'I wouldn't know. But the absolute cruellest thing you did, was not tell Marnie the truth about me. For all we know, the poor old woman thinks I was the victim sprawled on the train tracks. Do you have any remorse?'

'Does it all matter in the end, my first queen of hearts?' he said. 'After all, you gleefully accepted that gem and wad of cash.'

'Forcibly, Jarrod, forcibly. I was drugged remember!'

'No, no I don't. I remember a fabulous night of passion which led to me becoming a father. And the rest they say is history!' his chuckle cooling the balmy air.

'You're a sick man. If I had my younger legs, I'd have run from here long ago. But you had that deterrent built into this crazy plan, didn't you?'

'You have to admit, it's pretty bloody amazing! Look how far we have come and look how far we have gone back. The two eras are working beautifully. We still have cash, and trade healthily. Greed and the want of other Lands goes back centuries. All the corrupt government officials banned to their own sinking pit of bile, picked off as target practice for archers, barbarians and the wandering islanders who have an inherited hang-up.'

'What's worse? Marnie's obsession? Or yours?'

Jarrod switched arms causing Zessi to gasp in fright and splutter, 'Hell! I thought you were going to toss me into the moat!'

'Never! Soon you will be upright, and idolised for years to come. Minus the gem.'

'Obviously. Not much good it'll be when I'm dead.'

'Preserved. The word is preserved,' Jarrod hissed.

'What about Marnie?'

'Nah, she's to blame for Mum and Dad's demise.'

Zessi struggled. 'Put me down and leave me here to rot! You're an absolute beast to blame your dear little sister for that! How could you . . .?'

'Easily. Besides, she has one last performance . . .'

Again, Zessi struggled until she was able to rest her hand over Jarrod's mouth. 'No. I meant, how could you not tell her I'm here?'

He gently removed her hand. 'Let's enjoy our last night together, together.'

'You were the one who should have been on stage, Jarrod.'

'It's being fabricated as we speak. Hush now.'

***

Damon mentally ran through the checklist. Eyes confirmed his memorised checklist. Dry ice? Made. Temperature? Set. Tubes? Ready. Surgical tools? On the tray. Herb? In hand.

Everything was ready. Time to lock up and pay an old friend a visit.

***

'The conservatory?' Marnie muttered. 'How the hell did I get here?'

Little girl memory guided her to the French doors. Pushing them open, she stepped through, and breathed deeply. 'Oh, fresh air! How I love thee!'

A sound from behind caught her unaware.

'Maid Marnie?' said Jeeves, 'You shouldn't be out here.'

Dramatically turning, she gushed, 'I am Miss Marnie, and I have every right to be here. This is also my home. May I have some coffee please?'

Stepping out from behind him, a strapping lad of about eleven, mimicked. 'May I have some coffee please?' and ran away laughing.

'Who was that?'

'My grandson. Probably scabbing something from the kitchen.'

'Sounds like a marvellous idea, I would like something to eat too. But I don't scab. Nobody scabs these days. Don't you feed the children? Please tell me there are children and this isn't some exclusive adults orgy haven!'

'There are children, who at this time of night, should all be at home and in bed. Not this one, he's a right real rogue.'

Marnie smiled sweetly. 'So, what's in the kitchen?'

She led the way and ended up in the billiard room. 'This was over on the other side of the dining room.'

'Yes. Lord Jarrod redesigned the interior, and insisted the original kitchen and section above became a part of his private retreat. Follow me, I'll take you to the new one. It's bigger, brighter and very modern.'

Already hoeing into a sandwich, the lad tipped up a bottle of jam. Nothing dropped out.

'Tony! Finished another bottle, have you?' Jeeves uttered amid a broad grin.

Marnie smirked, 'Takes after you, I gather?'

'Will you take your coffee in the dining room, Maid Marnie?'

'Just call me Marnie! No, I will take it to my room, thank you.'

'I'll carry it for you,' Tony said excitedly.

'You know children are not allowed to play indoors at night,' reminded Jeeves, 'But seeing as there's a right real celebration going on over yonder, as long as you don't tell the others?'

'Thanks Pops, I promise I won't. I'll sneak into your quarters after.'

Tony slapped on the kettle and lit the gas. 'It's a whistler! So old. So cool! Reckon it's about as old as you Miss Marnie!'

His mischievous grin warmed her heart. 'Best bring some biscuits too seeing as you ate all the jam!'

Chuckling, Tony led her to a wooden kitchen chair and whispered into her ear as she sat. 'Looks like you're wearing an armoured plate under your dress. Are you meant to be at the party?'

She whispered back. 'No party, no plate. Do you know who I am?'

A mellow whistle burst through the air. 'Sweet and strong?' Jeeves asked.

'And white, thank you! May I have it in a mug, please?'

Tony piped up. 'Isn't it a bit late for coffee?'

'When you get to my age, you can do whatever, whenever and however. As long as its legal!'

'Oki-doki. Can you carry the biscuits?' He handed her a metal rectangle tin.

With its faded floral design surrounding a little girl wearing an apron, Marnie's eyes filled with tears. 'Mum's shortbread tin!' she whispered, pried open the lid and bit back a loud sob.

'Lord Jarrod is big on tradition,' Jeeves said quietly. 'Your coffee is ready. Kitchen is closed. Tony, this lady has had a big day so be mindful of the time, please.'

The lad grinned, helped Marnie to stand, made sure the biscuit tin was secure, and put a saucer over the lip of her mug. 'Let's go!'

Along the way, he described his love of the billiard room and the library. Beyond the elevator wall, was a darkened hallway. Marnie walked towards it.

'Not that way. We are not permitted to go beyond the lifts.'

'It's my house.'

Wide-eyed, Tony trembled, 'It's a scary section. I hate it. They don't come out the same. Besides, your coffee is getting cold. Let's go.'

***

He waited until their voices had diminished. Jeeves' back was still turned as he stepped out of the pantry.

'Is that who I think it is?'

'Dammit Damon! Don't do dat,' Jeeves spluttered and laughed.

He joined in. 'She's looking okay for her age too!

'Yeah, pretty chatty considering her indignation earlier!'

'Jeeves me old mate, once an actress, always an actress . . . always remember that!' Damon popped something into his mouth.

'What are you doing here anyway?'

'Well, Jarrod's bringing Zessi in tonight before she retires and he'll be looking to top up his energy beforehand. I recommend brewing a white ginger beverage.' Damon held out a paper-wrapped tuberous root. 'Here you go. It's better chewed, but he won't be into that.'

Jeeves frowned. 'What's going to happen with Marnie?'

'We'll just have to wait and see.' Damon checked the time. 'Right, things to do. Night Jeeves!'

He didn't wait for a reply, swung the tea-towels aside, depressed a button and slipped through the gap in the fake wall of the butler's pantry. The stonewall tunnel pleasantly scented and cool. Sensor lights lit the path as it wound its way around the western turret. Damon's dwelling veered off to the left, but tonight, he was expected somewhere else. Whistling a happy tune, he climbed the steps and rapped three times on the wooden door before pulling it open. Awaiting him, his bevvy of beauties. He didn't find the three-handed dwarfs ugly at all.

# Changes

Startled, Marnie awoke with an aching head full of tales of yore, modern times, and Jarrod's peculiarities, all jumbled with her father's voice. It took a while to realise why she felt something was jabbing her ribcage. At the foot of her bed curled up on the blanket box, Tony.

'Hey, sleepy head! The sun's coming up. You best get going before you're missed!'

He yawned, stretched, huffed and puffed. Then opened his eyes. 'Far out! Remember to turn the key if you don't want visitors. See ya.'

The lad hustled out like he'd been carried by a rocket. Her aching bones moved surprisingly quicker than they had for a while. After securing her suite, she pulled out the dress's elasticised waist and sighed loudly as the articles fell to the floor. That's when she remembered the note. Digging frantically in her pockets, she retrieved the slip of paper. RUN AWAY.

'To where?' she demanded of the empty room.

Soothed by the scent of lavender and running water, Marnie turned to the third last page of the journal.

*Together the pieces be, or apart, you will always own my heart. Love Dad.*

'That's all very well, Dad, but you also told me all this ends with me,' she murmured. 'How? Do I put on another performance with the journal and hair pin strapped to my body and be the one to perish in the fire?'

The sound of a jingling telephone disturbed her thoughts. Frowning, she padded through to her bedroom, hid the treasures under her pillow and answered the telephone sitting on the writing desk.

'Hello?'

'Jeeves here. Your breakfast has been riding between the storeys. Do you not care for it?' There was a distinct coolness to his voice.

'You sound like you had a bad night. Thanks for the thought, but it's a little early for me. I shall be down in a while and have breakfast in the conservatory.'

'It'll be closer to brunch by then.'

Marnie smirked. 'Suits me,' and hung up. Thought better of the idea, lifted off the handpiece and placed it gently on the table.

Submerged to her neck in the bathtub, through blurred eyes watched the bubbles fly off her hand as she waved it regally. Marnie began the old story and hoped for the best.

***

Jarrod lowered Zessi onto the inflatable mattress. Like a million hands supporting her body, thick warm liquid provided perfect buoyancy. His rubber gloved hands parted her thinning grey hair, caressed her face then fluttered around her belly button.

He spoke gently. 'You'll be forever asleep before the water gets a lot colder, my first queen of hearts.'

'And you'll get back what is yours after all these years.'

'That is true. The best hiding place . . .'

'You were damn lucky those scoundrels didn't recognise me after they killed Valentino.'

'They did their job well.'

'Yeah, scared us enough to make us leave so we never found out the truth. . .well, Marnie anyway.'

'You always knew the bloke played more than one role in all of this, but like a good girl, you kept another secret.'

'It's not my guilt that's killing me, Jarrod.'

He kissed her. Hard and long. He only stopped when her face turned crimson.

'Did she ever see the jewel?' he demanded.

Barely audible, Zessi said, 'No, knew nothing about us . . . or a child. It'll break . . . her heart . . .'

A shaft of red light briefly illuminated the doorway. Damon breezed in. 'Morning all, I see we have our VIP ready and waiting.'

'She's fading fast, let's get on with it.'

Zessi struggled to sit up. Water sloshed and splashed until Jarrod inserted a needle into the side of her neck.

'Stop it! No water allowed on the floor!' Damon said firmly. 'Relax Zes, it'll all be over soon.'

'Promise you'll . . . tell her . . . please.'

Simultaneously, the men hushed her. Then continued with their own conversation while configuring the heart-lung resuscitator, confirming data outputs and preparing the ice bath.

'I do think the chain of life should be a witness to this,' Damon said.

'No. There is no guarantee once they see all the chambers they'd keep their mouths closed. No matter how much we manipulate their memories.'

'The mind, Jarrod. We manipulate the mind. Only the Yanks manipulate memories. Marnie's the example of that remember?' Damon scoffed. 'Right, ready when you are to run through the chemical formulae.'

'Chemicals?' Zessi moaned.

'Calculated specific to your body mass to prevent the stomach lining from dissolving.' On a roll, Damon continued to explain the process. 'Then your blood is drained, replaced by a preserving solution for your organs. Eventually an antifreeze is injected to protect the cells . . .'

Suddenly, the sensor of the heart monitor alerted them to a failing organ.

'No, no, no,' Jarrod cried.

'Can't use the defrib, mate!'

'Pull her out, pull her out.'

A morbid endless monotone filled the room. Jarrod's legs wouldn't move.

Damon slapped his mate's face. 'You will lose Zessi's organs forever if you do not move her now.'

'But . . .'

Damon scooped up the body, put it into Jarrod's arms, and shouted, 'Move! We need chemicals in and blood out. Come on, Jarrod. Snap out of it! There's still time!'

Afterwards, they stood either side and recited their farewell intone. 'Thank you for your donation to medical science. May you be the one to save a life.'

As was custom after a gruelling episode, they dialled into their overseas cohorts, cross-referenced and exchanged data, discussed upcoming projects to meet quotas, then retreated to their respective offices. Alarms set, they inhaled their soothing concoction and reclined their lounges.

***

Feeling adventurous after not dying in the bathtub, Marnie decided the servant's elevator would be a good start to her adventure. Journal secured around her aged midriff and hair pin hanging to her navel, satisfied too that the baggy granny-dress was the perfect disguise, she clutched her favourite hat and set off.

Turning the key to access the facilities, inside the stainless-steel compartment a whole new world greeted her when the doors slid closed. Engraved into the panels, a map of The Kingdom of Jalekem. Suppressing a scoff, her index finger automatically followed the trail from beyond the kitchen to the layout of the community. Jarrod's take on medieval urban logic, summed up the man himself. Controlling. Plum centre of what was her favourite garden, a building marked by a spire. Her eye was drawn to the only marked buildings. The stable and blacksmith's forge. Most peculiarly, steps led to a door within an unravelling circle.

'What on earth?' Marnie mumbled. 'It looks like a stretched slinky.'

Screwing up her eyes, she saw that it uncurled its way through the fallow field and beyond the village green.

'Ooh! It's a tunnel,' she exclaimed delightedly, finger-walked its path until it split in two. 'And another one! Oh, this one follows along the moat, then alongside the aqueduct and . . . beyond the gate. Freedom!'

Marnie pressed the open button, slipped off a shoe to keep the doors apart, tottered back to her bag and retrieved a biro. While there, replaced the handset and patted it gently. She really did love the French style old-fashioned telephone. When the elevator doors slid closed, she paid closer attention to the interior of the manor. The majority of its layout was how she remembered her childhood home, added to what Jeeves had explained about the kitchens, her focus was on what had changed.

Annoyed because she felt she was wasting time and had to almost get undressed, hoped there weren't any cameras, hitched up her dress, unravelled the makeshift strapping and removed the journal. Several pages past her father's sentiment, Marnie quickly drew a mud-map. A stop-sign symbol had been etched into a new hallway running parallel to the drawing room. The new room, a bulging square beyond the exterior of the manor, was untidily scratched out. As if a child was still learning to colour in. On the outer wall and adjacent to, a cross-hatched rectangle marked: *Generator Room*. An inswing door led to a construction symbolised by a 3D cube snowflake. She had seen enough.

# Surprises

Jeeves watched, waited, and kept whisking. The elevator hadn't budged off her floor. He knew the old woman was going to be trouble the moment she spoke. Glancing at the time, he also knew he was not to wake Lord Jarrod, or all hell would break loose. With the egg whites perfectly aerated and seasoned, the asparagus and prosciutto sautéed, golden foamy butter ready and waiting, he poured the critical ingredients of his famous fluffy omelette into the pan. After a count of 10 seconds, tapped it to burst any air bubbles, sprinkled half with the sauteed topping and a sprinkling of pecorino, and slipped the pan into the pre-heated oven.

As the elevator doors opened, he mumbled under his breath, 'Woman could probably hear a kettle being boiled from a mile away too.'

'Oh, Jeeves!' Marnie gushed as she waltzed into the kitchen, 'Is that for me?'

'First of all, you are to use your own elevator, and secondly, I will bring you something to eat in the conservatory as you wished.'

'That will be lovely.'

She bustled out the door, and headed towards the no-go zone.

From behind her, a quiet voice. 'That's not the way, Miss Marnie.'

She jumped, turned around a little bit too quickly and teetered. 'You startled me! Not a good idea for a woman of my age.'

'Nor is going down there,' Tony replied, held her hand firmly and ushered her in the right direction.

Deciding that a view of the land would be a more pleasant vista, the lad helped Marnie get comfortable at the dining room in time for Jeeves to enter with a loaded trolley. 'Lad, I forgot the tea tray, if you wouldn't mind.'

The moment Tony was out of ear shot, with a flourish Jeeves positioned a domed plate in front of her. Mirth twinkled in his eyes, yet his mouth was in a tight line. 'Brunch is served! Do not lead each other astray, Marnie. He's a good story teller and you're a good actress. A very dangerous combination, and something we can't have at the moment.'

'Really? Do tell!' Marnie said theatrically.

Jeeves lifted the lid. 'Would rather you eat this before it sinks.'

'Oh yum! Won't you sit with me a while?'

Tony announced his arrival rather loudly, deposited the tray on the dining table and bowed deeply. 'Lady Marnie! That's what you should be called, and Pops, I've decided I am going to petition Lord Jarrod for a stage!'

'You and whose army?' the older man challenged.

'Us kids! Maybe some of the dwarves! We need some fun too! Besides, we could dedicate it to the first queen of . . .'

Jeeves shot him a look that would take out a fly in the next room.

'Dwarves?' Marnie said, wide-eyed. 'I love those little beings! Can I see them?'

For the second time, Tony's eyes conveyed a message of terror.

Marnie turned and started with fright. Jarrod and Damon walked briskly straight past the glassed room; heads bowed in hushed conversation. Their black cloaks flapping like wings.

'Morning Jarrod, nice to see you again Damon!' she called out.

'Hush, they are not to be interrupted,' Jeeves snapped. 'Tony, go back to the village and make yourself useful.'

The lad didn't hesitate, took off his shoes, jumped onto the window seat, pushed open an easement, sat on the sill, put his shoes back on and simply disappeared.

Marnie swallowed a mouthful of the delicious savoury airiness, positioned another piece onto her fork. 'What's all the fuss about? They're just men. Humans. People. Why are you walking on eggshells?'

Flummoxed, Jeeves hastily poured her a cup of tea and bid her adieu. Moments later, he returned and stood beside her. In a quiet voice, said, 'About three or four years ago, Tony used to push Kevan and Leanna along the garden paths. Together or alone, they filled his head with a lot of nonsense about ancient curses, murderers, freaks, theatre fires and early medical experiments. Being so young in the mind, he had nightmares. It took ages to convince him the stories were just that. But one day, not so long ago, he went exploring into places he shouldn't go. Ever since, is terrified of those two men.'

'And you protect him,' Marnie said gently.

'He's my surrogate grandson. There was a construction accident, resulting in him becoming an orphan.'

'Is that what happened to your leg?'

'No. Keep eating, please.' He spoke quickly and quietly. 'After the tragic death of the only two people in the world I had ever cared about, I was left with not much hope. I had heard of Jarrod's eccentricity so I volunteered to have a robotic surgeon design, programme and construct me a brand-new leg. They also reconstructed my brain. Mainly human, part robot. It was a ground-breaking experiment to not have human interaction. I was one of the lucky ones though. There's a reason humans need humans.'

'I'm fascinated Jeeves, care to tell me more?'

'No. There's a button inside the walk-in robe which automatically concertinas the wall panel revealing the section of the suite you're familiar with minus the balcony. From there, you can see the village. The folk are very protective of what's theirs.'

'And mine.'

'That's not quite correct,' Jarrod stated flatly and wheeled the trolley away from the table.

'Hell man! Do you want to give me a heart attack?' Marnie almost choked.

'Jeeves, some food and coffee please. Damon's joining us.'

The butler nodded and left the room without another word.

'Good morning, Jarrod. Hell of an entrance! You sure you haven't been on stage before?'

'Ha! That's funny,' Damon said, squeezed her shoulder and kissed the top of her head. 'Hello Mar, nice to see you again. It's been a while!'

Blushing, she waited until she could see him properly. 'Hasn't it! You aged well, Damon, what's your secret?'

'Bit of this and a bit of that! Your brother makes a very nice mead.'

The men sat opposite each other.

Marnie patted her forehead. 'Of course! It should have dawned on me earlier you'd be brewing some medieval beverage. Still tinkering with letter openers by chance?' she flicked Jarrod a belittling look.

He sniggered. 'Most of us have grown up since then. Tell me something, would you dare put on another performance?'

Instantly, Marnie's eyes filled with tears.

'Sorry, little sister, that wasn't necessary. I had a bad night which is no excuse for my rudeness.'

She bit her lip and nodded her head.

Damon interjected. 'Mar, how about I ask you? Our village folk have never really been entertained by someone in your field. Amateur music, yes, but not the telling of a story. Let's keep it simple. A few props. A stage. Your narration.'

Jeeves deposited one platter of buttery, flaky croissants and another with a variety of condiments in front of them. She caught his eye.

'My omelette was the best I've ever had, thank you. Glad I wore this baggy dress, because I cannot resist one of those.'

He smiled dutifully at her, then looked at Jarrod. 'If you don't need me for anything else, Lord?'

'Hang on a moment.' Jarrod took particular care in coating the exterior of the largest croissant with rosella jam. Poised before his mouth, said, 'I know, I know, not the proper way to eat these things, but it's how I like to eat them! Anyway, let's get your opinion on Maid Marnie telling an old fable. What say you? Hmm, Jeeves?'

Pan faced, he shifted his weight from his unreal leg to the other, breathed in deeply, and said, 'A marvellous idea indeed.'

'That's settled then. Thanks Jeeves, that will be all for now.'

'My Lord, Damon.'

Marnie couldn't resist and mimicked her brother, then cackled uncontrollably. 'You're the one who's living in an unreal world! Gawd, do you hear yourself, big brother?'

'Actually, Mar, this is Jarrod's kingdom. His land. Legally.'

'Righto,' she rolled her eyes. 'I will not live here confined to my suite, so I will be returning to my villa in Venice next week. Yes, I will do one performance. It should be at night time. Add a curtain to the list of requirements.'

Jarrod applauded. 'Excellent. Will tomorrow night be too soon?'

'Be fair to the people!'

'Okay. The night afterwards then. It's a quiet time in the village, so this will give them something to do. Rather excellent, I say.'

Marnie pushed back her chair and turned to leave. 'If you'll excuse me, I've got things to do.'

'You're excused,' Jarrod said, spraying crumbs into his serviette, 'Might see if we can rustle up some VIPs for you!'

'No, please don't. The holograms creeped me out at the funeral.' She had her head lowered when she replaced her chair under the table, and didn't see the look that passed between Jarrod and Damon before she shuffled out the room.

'You didn't?' Damon admonished.

'Yeah, couldn't resist creating a last waltz. I do feel a bit bad about it now, though.'

'Good.'

Jeeves entered silently, cleared the table, poured the coffees and updated the men on the data received from their cohorts. 'In summary, all parties are satisfied.'

Damon said, 'Bravo! Later today, can you arrange for my den to be sanitised?'

'Of course.

'Did you see her?' Jarrod asked with a grin.

'Yes, heading towards the elevator having a good old conversation with herself.'

He simply nodded his head, then issued carrot-dangling tasks for Jeeves to take to the people.

'Perhaps do that now, then come back and tidy up?'

He bowed slightly and pushed open the French doors.

'Be sure to build excitement!' Jarrod called after him.

Damon suggested it was time to check on the future custodians of the Kingdom.

Barely containing his excitement, Jarrod said, 'Great idea! I need your input on the position of the unlocking key. Let's go!'

***

Instead of returning to her suite, Marnie had walked through the kitchen and caught Tony helping himself to some little pies. Like naughty kids, they snuck into the pantry and devoured a couple more. Eventually the lad's smirk, quickly lost when he stuffed another one into his gob, beckoned rapidly with his free hand for her to follow. Marnie caught up to him just as he let the tea-towels fall back into place. Together they stepped into the tunnel.

'You have to be quiet,' Tony whispered. 'The first thing you're going to see is not nice. But when we get to the other side, you'll be happy. It was Kevan's favourite reading place.'

Too stunned to speak, she let him take her hand. Thankful for the lit walkway, with her spare hand, felt the walls. 'How old is this tunnel?'

'Dunno. Kevan said it had something to do with Leanna's side and he was never allowed to talk about it. So, we didn't. He was good like that. I could tell him heaps of stuff and he would tell me heaps of stuff. Our secrets. You remind me of him.'

Tony stopped abruptly, put his ear to the wall, then put his finger to his mouth. He cracked an unseen door jamb just enough for them to poke their heads through the gap. Marnie's legs buckled.

'Scary huh? Come on, let's go before we're trapped and end up like them!'

'Lead the way, I'm going to puke.'

Gulping in the fresh air, Tony helped Marnie sit on timber bench, and practically sat on her lap. 'Look into the pond. Count the fish. Breathe. That's what Kevan told me to do. It helps, I promise.'

After a long while, Marnie was confident only words were going to come out of her mouth when it opened, and said, 'Why do you call them by their first names? Not mister or missus, aunt or uncle or heaven forbid, Lord and Lady?'

Tony giggled. 'I only called them great grandad and grandmother when it was just us. Kevan was a great actor. Leanna, she was . . . um . . . not sly, that's harsh . . . more like wily. We used to play games with Pops and the other elders when we were in their company . . . seeing who could trip up the other. None of us did! Your parents weren't as thick as they made out either.'

'Oh?'

'No. They didn't always take their medicine. I miss them. Do you?'

Tears suddenly welled up in Marnie's eyes. Did she? Did she really know how to grieve?

'It's not a hard question,' Tony jumped up and stomped away.

He disappeared through a hedged archway and appeared opposite her. With the pond between him, he tossed pebbles at her. Every now and then, she'd get splashed. Eventually finding some underneath the bench, she collected a handful and returned fire. Tony beckoned her over, and pointed the way silently. When she did see him again, he was sitting atop a flat rock with a grubby glassed cupboard built into its wall.

'A library?'

'Yeah! Kevan's and my stash. Not even Leanna knew about this hidey-hole. Look around, nobody can see us!'

He was right. Behind them, the wall of the manor's turret stood like a sentry, in front of them a towering hedge, and above, fickle clouds played with the sun.

Tony tugged at her hand. 'We would take turns in reading to each other. I love the smell of books, holding them, hugging them when something you've read makes you feel happy or sad. Fiction is great, but fact is where I learn things about brainwaves and telekinesis. I even have a hiding place in the library. If you stay long enough I'll show you. Anyway, Kevan gave me all his books which I've hidden, except one. It's still in there.'

'You haven't taken it?'

Shaking his head, Tony unlatched the door. 'Because the thing's got your name on it.'

He stepped back and let Marnie retrieve a small book-sized timber box. Carved into the lid, an auspicious shape. No matter what they tried, it just wouldn't open. Marnie suddenly gasped.

'What is it?'

'I need to return to my suite. I ate far too many apple pies.'

Tony snorted with laughter and latched the door closed. He fussed about with the orange trumpet vine, then said, 'We'll take the servants elevator. We can access it from outside. Fingers crossed Pops is busy elsewhere!'

Marnie chewed the inside of her cheek. 'If I can hold on long enough, reckon you could show me where the generator is?'

The poor lad's face paled significantly. 'Not today. Please, not today.'

She winked reassuringly, then smirked, 'I don't think I can hold on anyway!'

***

Jarrod lounged silently against the doorjamb while Damon scratched around in his drawer for another loupe, muttering under his breath.

Eventually, he held out the tatty box. 'Found it! Mate, that's not an African diamond, nor one of ours. I'm telling you, if it came from your mother's side in Europe, it'll be Brazilian. And if it is, Zessi was walking around with a multi-million jewel which kept her navel taught. I can't believe your mother never missed it! But I'm even more surprised Zessi never hocked it!'

Jarrod smirked. 'I'm not. Told her she'd bleed out if she tried to remove it.'

Damon shook his head. 'You're a cruel bastard.'

'But smart?'

Exasperated, replied, 'Yep. A smart, cruel bastard.'

Standing over the control panel, Damon confirmed his opinion and using a bezel setting, carefully applied pressure with the flat-end pusher to bend the prongs over the magnificent gem, securing it against the ring. At his instruction, Jarrod soldered the wire into place on the bypass lighting circuit.

'If the beacon above the available cryostats glow, we know we're on the right path for handing over to the future! You ready, Jarrod?'

The men shook hands. 'Yes, yes I am!'

Hands overlapping; they were just about to turn the gem-key as Jeeves opened the door carrying a dwarf. 'Damon, you have a problem.'

'Tippy, no! What happened?'

'I found her half way out of your room, looks like she panicked and I don't carry around sniffing salts. I have to attend to the others now. Here you go, this belongs to you.' Jeeves handed over the bundle and rushed out the door.

'Dammit all to hell,' Jarrod raged. 'Bloody Marnie! I bet she's been sniffing around.'

***

Her suite locked off to the world, Marnie ignored the jingling telephone by shutting the door to the walk-in robe. Nestled into the lid of the box, the copper hair pin. On the dresser atop the old journal, sat the fabric covered booklet authored by her father, outlining the memory suppression in her youth, his courier job for some of the worlds' largest university science labs, and the consequences if spoken about such topics. His biggest regret was fostering the obsessions each child had involuntarily adopted. Marnie noted his handwriting varied with the entries, the latest being the scrappiest. It matched RUN AWAY.

Covering the top of her dressing table, an A3 schematic of Jarrod's private spaces identifying their access points and pin codes. On the reverse, a simple wiring diagram of how to override the generator, and the devastating effect it would have on all of Jalekem if she chose to.

'Why?' She cried, fanned the notepad in frustration. 'How does it all end with me?'

It was at that moment Marnie remembered Ox Cart Annie hid the list inside the mantelet's secret compartment. Using the pin, unpicked several tacking stitches until the notepad sat bare. There weren't any seams. No secret compartments.

'Think, Marnie, think,' she told herself, tapped her forehead and stared at her reflection in the brightened vanity mirror. 'Of course!'

Compelled to hold the wrong side of the fabric to the mirror, Marnie took an age to decipher her father's handwriting. Eventually, she ran a bath. Not even the lavender soothed her qualms. Sobbing helplessly, Marnie had never felt so alone in her life.

Screaming as a million dwarves flew at her face, Marnie awoke in a lather of perspiration, flat bubbles and a cold bath. Incensed by the deception and the feeling of being left to cling onto the precipice of people's lives, she comforted herself by eating the last pieces of shortbread.

Still wide awake at midnight, Marnie watched the world below slumber under dancing firelight. Desperate to drink in the clear night air, try as she might, not one window opened. Giving in to her brother's eccentricity, a single tear slipped down her cheek as time stood still. Alloy-silver ribbons of moonlight shimmered on the moat creating an enormously beautiful necklace winding its way around a sleeping oligarchy.

It was as if Ox Cart Annie had somehow nudged Marnie from a different dimension. Whispered words fogged up the pane. 'I release you forthwith.'

***

Another baggy dress, treasures bound and hidden, and stockinged feet, Marnie stepped out of her elevator onto the ground floor. Turning right, she walked directly down the no-go hallway, felt along the wall. Deemed from the schematic that it wasn't an obvious doorway, guesstimated the steps per metre. A miniscule bump in the panelling hid the recessed pin code panel. Backlit buttons made her life easier and after a subtle beep, the door slid open. She blindly stepped inside.

'Mar?'

'Damon!'

'How the hell . . .?

'What on earth . . .?'

She staggered backwards. Damon caught her before she fell.

'Let me go this minute.'

'Not on your Nelly. . . let me show you what happens to people who sneak around.'

He forced her onto a backless stool with wheels and used her shoulders to steer them to a darkened section. Several female adolescents sat at sewing machines. Others painted on masks. Male adolescents soldered motherboards. Behind them, Jeeves bolted mannequins together. He looked up, blinked, brushed something out of his eyes, and returned to the task at hand.

'They're mostly kids! They should be in bed asleep . . . '

'Yet, here they are!' Damon affirmed.

'Is this some sort of sick punishment? And Jeeves? Doesn't he do enough around here?' Marnie looked around the area. 'And you've used the casino lighting effect. That's just plain cruel.'

'The what?'

'The casino lighting effect. Tricking patrons to lose track of time by blocking out the windows and using artificial lighting. You're messing with these kids' body clocks. Isn't that illegal?'

'You have no idea what has transpired over the years, Mar, but one thing I will tell you is that Jeeves is the prototype for the future. He agreed to it . . .'

'What? His leg?' Marnie said, incredulously.

'You always were smarter than you made out to be but you can't fool me. Although I feel I must warn you for this next section. It's probably Jarrod's favourite.'

'I hope my heart is strong enough.'

'So do I,' Damon said.

He positioned the stool alongside a smaller pane with a ledge, almost a server's window. A large frosted panel extended beyond. As if by magic, it cleared. A series of robots sat with their backs to them, while a lad affixed old-fashioned nurses' hats with ebony wigs onto the shiny domes. He moved like a robot himself. Yet it was his stature that had Marnie enthralled.

'That's Tony! What have you done to him?'

'Hypnotism. Jarrod's very good at it. But you already know that, don't you Mar?'

She chortled. 'When?'

'On your way home.'

'No. I slept. Anyway, what's with the robot-looking nurses? Another fanciful notion?'

Instead of answering her, Damon slid the small pane upwards and called out 'Attention. Attention. Very slowly, you will rotate 90 degrees.'

Tony still attempted to position the accessories when the robots swivelled. It didn't matter the items dropped, or the robots' knees collided with his. He just kept on doing what he was made to do.

'Oh Tony, I'm sorry,' Marnie whispered.

'I know you saw my dwarves too,' Damon said quietly. 'And you took the biscuit tin.'

His hand covered her mouth before she got a chance to reply. He ordered the robots to stop and smile. Sixteen pair of emotionless, wide eyes bore deep into Marnie's soul. There was only one person who could smile so beautifully. Marnie thrashed her head about, screamed against his hand.

Warm breath tickled both ears. Two very familiar voices spoke in unison. 'Yes, they are all Zessi. Soon to have her happier memories.'

Jarrod commanded the robots to arise and approach. They did. Marnie struggled desperately to stand up, until he spoke again.

'Now, my dear little sister, come and see something else.'

Damon pressed his hand harder against Marnie's mouth, and said, 'Jarrod, she's not ready to see . . . '

'No. Not that. I recreated her very first performance . . . you both remember that don't you? Anyway, I introduced some elements of the old fable too. But the grand finale is what is really brilliant. Brilliant!' he sang. 'A great accompaniment to her last performance tomorrow night. Actually, tonight! Tomorrow is today!'

'We never discussed this!' Damon retorted.

'Funny that. You never told me you would keep the failures. We're even. Follow me.'

A particularly uncomfortable veil settled over them. Marnie shrank. Damon propped her up and whispered in her ear, 'I'll get you out of here. Don't speak.' He waited until she nodded, then removed his hand.

A stage was projected onto the floor. The back of their parents' heads and a side profile of the old man beside the stage came into focus, with the rest of the audiences' heads blurred. Suddenly, a young girl appeared on a chair centre stage. A metallic object gained momentum as it rolled from the wings and slammed up against her ankles. Smoke wound itself around the chair and danced behind her until it contorted into the shape of Jalekem's crest. The curtains burst into flame. The audience turned. Zooming images of Zessi's smiling face pulsated, until they morphed into one single picture. She was holding a baby.

'The end,' Jarrod said. He pulled Marnie off the stool and gripped her shoulders firmly. 'You disappoint me with your sneaking around, then you befriend someone whose mental state is already compromised. As punishment, you shall perform while Jalekem feasts.'

Marnie didn't dare speak as Jarrod pushed her back down.

Damon steadied her, asked the begging question. 'And who is to escort the star of the show this time?'

'I shall with my canines. And you, my friend, do not show any further leniency to my sister.'

Jarrod hummed the soothing melody, one handed rhythmically tapped his thigh, the other hand cupped his sister's chin.

In a quiet tone, said, 'Shut your eyes, open your mind and close your mouth.'

Before long, her breathing slowed and he spoke normally. 'I'll take her back to her suite. Damon, prep another four chambers.'

A long silence ensued.

'Senior Medical Scientist Damon?'

It had been a very long time since he had heard the threatening tone. He knew how best to respond. 'Yes, yes of course, Lord Jarrod.'

# Let The Show Begin!

'Time to rise and shine!' Jeeves sung out from the elevator. 'It's almost midday, and you need to eat and hydrate.'

Snuffling into her pillow, Marnie squeezed her eyes tightly and screwed up lips until they touched nose. Percolated coffee beans permeating the air encouraged her face to relax.

'It's too early,' she mumbled.

'Come along now. Brunch is ready. You eat, I'll talk, we've got lots to get through.'

Resistance was futile. Before she knew it, Marnie was propped up, surrounded by pillows with a laden tray beside her on the bed. Draped over the blanket box, a green mantelet and other costumery.

'Boy, you sure kicked up a stink! I thought you were a figment of my imagination at first, but then I saw the movie reel. I've hidden Tony for his and your sakes.' Jeeves handed her a mug of freshly brewed coffee and tutted quietly. 'Jarrod is behaving rather abnormally and Damon is spending an unusual amount of time in the lab with Tippy and few of the others.'

Marnie snuck a look under the silver dome, smiled. 'Oh Jeeves! Eggs Benedict, bet that's homemade Hollandaise sauce, ooh is that salmon?'

'Of course. In case it's your last meal!'

'In case?'

'Yes. Now eat up, and please listen carefully.'

Jeeves sat in a reading chair with this back to the wall between the high windows. From his pocket, he pulled out a notepad. It was bound in the same fabric Marnie had unpicked from hers. He hushed her by putting his finger up to his mouth. When he spoke, his voice was that of someone very old from a different time.

'I am constructed out of several people. Part of my human mind is that of your grandfather who taught Jarrod everything he knows about an ancient craft and era. That man is the same old man who sat beside the stage and left you some very important items of which must never see the light of day, ever again.'

Enchanted, Marnie used her finger to wipe dripping egg yolk off her chin and nodded encouragingly. Jeeves continued.

'As young men, Jarrod and Damon dared to push the extremes in experimentation, courtesy of your father's connections, and, fearfully because of your mother's connections. Yes, both sets of forebearers dabbled in the theatre in one way or another. But during the First and Second World Wars, science began to play an important role.'

Jeeves unscrewed his leg. In the recess of where a calf muscle would ordinarily reside, he pulled out a photograph. It was the first time Marnie had seen a face crumple. After a long while, it returned to normal. He replaced the keepsake and explained that Jarrod and Damon were responsible for increasing the kingdom's population and its selected residents. Both brilliant men in many ways, including manipulating cells to prevent ocular diseases. Their futuristic ideals with sustainability, own organic produce and isolation would put them in good standing for longevity. Ongoing medical science practices and knowledge would eventually see the revival of preserved humans and animals, thereby forward-thinking evolution.

'So, they practice cryonics?'

'No. It is believed they have perfected cryonics.'

Marnie shook her head. 'Delicious brunch, yet again, thanks Jeeves!' and wriggled out of bed without disturbing the tray.

The butler turned towards the window and sighed. 'You saw my face crumple like a baby?'

'Yes. Please tell me they didn't programme your head to fall off if you laughed too hard!'

'That's right, they didn't. But listen to this.' He wiped his hand over the front of his face, opened his mouth, and laughed every conceivable type of laugh,

Holding onto her belly, 'Enough! No more! My tummy hurts.'

'And what were you hiding under such a baggy dress, Marnie?'

In a blink of any eye, feigned indignation. 'Oh, not I, Jeeves. Will you tell me about the other part of your brain?'

'Better still, I'll show you.'

Jeeves pressed behind his right ear. A screen slid out from underneath his hairline and flipped open.

'Technology, eh?' he chuckled and dragged over another chair. 'Come sit beside me and I'll take you for a flying visit . . . just tell me what part of the manor you would like to see.'

Marnie didn't hesitate. 'The library, museum and where I was last night.'

It was if she were on the back of a bird. They swooped into the library, perched atop the mantelpiece, darted through the splendid chandelier, hovered around the crystal stopper on the sherry decanter and rested on her father's favourite reading chair. After her breath returned to normal, they continued. Squeezing through the keyhole into the museum; years of medieval armoury shone under a ceiling full of recessed downlights. Silver carafes, ceramic dinnerware and hemp sacks hung off the bow of an old sailing ship which protruded from a wall. Encased in a glass cabinet, the steel gorget, and above it in a beautiful ornate gold frame, the Title Deeds from the original acquisition to current day. Behind a stained-glass shopfront, an 1800s laboratory. On the solid bench, familiar trunks lay open displaying bottles and bottles of things suspended in liquid. Centre place beside a twisted goblet, the largest bottle of all. Preserved within and standing proudly; Ox Cart Annie's index finger.

Marnie shuddered.

'Embrace the actress,' Jeeves voice echoed in her ears. 'Last stop. Hold on.'

Suddenly, they were balanced on the top of the frosted window looking across the room. Zessi-robots educated pupils of all types, varying ages, in all subjects. In the back corner, Jarrod adjusted the temperature on a sealed room to –243$^{0}$C and pointed to Damon who threw his hands up in the air, then pointed back at Jarrod then at a rotating red light. They both dashed over to a dark room where massive cylinders stood upright. Marnie craned her neck and saw feet. In a blink of an eye, they dropped to slightly above floor level. There was Zessi sound asleep, greyed and of similar age, inverted, hands resting across her navel. Beside her; banks of canisters contained young and old preserved people. Half way along, a body was dissolving right in front of their very eyes.

'No . . . I can't stand any more of this. . .' Marnie muttered.

'You have to see something else to understand,' Jeeves said, and took their view upwards.

They hovered along the pipework until the third row. Very slowly, they slid down between two canisters. Marnie looked left and right, and wailed.

'What's to understand? Jarrod lied. He didn't do as Mum and Dad wished.'

The screen receded and Jeeves patted Marnie's hand. 'You need to fathom the complexity of this kingdom. It is a strange word for the year two thousand and thirty-four . . . but legally this is what it is called.'

She sighed loudly. 'And if he dies? Or Damon? Who runs the joint then?'

'The next generation of course! Just as it does everywhere else in the world.'

Staring out the window at the villagers going about their business like ants, Marnie pondered on his comment.

'And Tony? Will I see him again?'

Jeeves chortled, 'He's a rascal, who knows!'

***

Twelve sleek dogs sat in an arc with their backs to Jarrod. Their ears as upright as steel posts. The typical Doberman pinscher stance as fascinating as the literary Knights of the Round Table. Resembling Ox Cart Annie, Marnie bit back a smirk and deliberately shook and jutted out the green mantelet to stir up the novel welcoming party waiting for her in the conservatory. She jousted playfully with the hair pin at Jarrod.

'Not a good idea, Marnie. I'm not in a jovial mood,' he grumbled.

'Ah, come on dear big brother! Just for old times' sake?'

'While the dramas that unfolded overnight were not all of your doing, I'm still highly annoyed.'

'I don't recall. I just know I slept very heavily!' Marnie smiled demurely. 'Can we put all that aside and actually catch up before tonight's performance? We've hardly spoken since the limo ride! Nice dogs by the way. If you don't mind, I won't pat them.'

'Good idea. Let's go for a stroll.' He clicked his tongue twice. 'They'll lead the way.'

Glorious fiery tones infused the early twilight sky, painting the towering clouds with anticipation. Jarrod breathed deeply, exhaled loudly and casually draped his arm around Marnie's shoulder. The evening air scented with freshly mowed grass and sizzling spit-roast pigs, a welcome calming tonic.

'Life's funny, you know,' Jarrod said, 'Mum and Dad helped you follow your dreams which inadvertently led me to following mine. I always believed I was born in the wrong era. I desperately wanted to be a knight, but as I excelled in my career, a knight just wasn't going to cut it! I wanted it all. To be all. And when it's my time, I will go down in history as having seriously buggered up the history books and set the path for the future!'

Marnie chuckled, 'Mission accomplished, then?'

'Indeed!'

'You really ought to have told Mum about Grandad and the significance of the white swans.'

'What? What on earth are you talking about?'

'On the way back from their funeral, you told me . . .'

'I hypnotised you.'

'Did you?'

His laugh, hollow. 'Once an actress, always the actress, huh?'

Ahead, the dogs trotted in formation along the cobblestone path beside the aqueduct. In true professor-manner Jarrod described the intricacies of water reticulation, importance of sustainability, naturally insulated dwellings, and stopped midstride when a group of children squealed from the back of a wagon drawn by a mule.

'It's not?' Marnie scoffed.

'It is! Well, the best we could do given we don't have an ox.' Jarrod clapped his hands, the children silenced and scooted over to one side.

He gallantly lent his sister a hand and helped her settle on the raised wooden seat before taking his position beside her.

'Hello,' an adolescent boy said boldly. His stormy grey eyes blinked once, as slowly as an analogue camera that once would have captured a youthful Marnie on 35mm film. He stood up and bowed deeply. 'I am Delray, the first great-grandson of the first procreator. It is our pleasure to have you entertain us tonight.'

The laughter lines that framed Marnie's knowing eyes crinkled when she smiled her reply. 'Hello, and thank you.'

Jarrod prevented any further conversation by regaling tales from his youth as it entwined with his little sister's success. The waft of campfires and carved meat made Marnie's stomach rumble. Silently, she cussed Jeeves for not allowing her to have an early dinner. His after-performance promise of a platter of roast pork, apple sauce and vegetables felt as far away as Venice. Most of the children jumped from the cart as it neared the back of a makeshift stage in between two haystacks, and ran away hooting and hollering their excitement. Delray bowed his head, alighted with childlike agility then commanded the dogs to follow him as he raced after his friends. A sooty smell wafted across the fabric runners strung across a large beam. Jarrod helped the star of the show descend and steered her towards the stage steps, pausing momentarily to pop something into his mouth.

'Why did you not feel you could tell me the truth about Zessi?' Marnie asked quietly.

'It wasn't your business,' he said, rolled his shoulders.

'What about her baby? Plus, you ignored Mum and Dad's wishes. Why?'

Jarrod blinked rapidly as if to quell the sudden onset of tears. He faked a sneeze into a monogrammed green and white handkerchief. 'Pardon me, I feel something got up my nose.'

'Answer the questions, Jarrod. Was the baby Damon's or yours? Then tell me why you lied to me, then after that, tell me who belongs to the ashes resting in that gorget! I mean, really? Whose funeral slash memorial did I attend?'

'You need to stop prying and get on with the show.' Flickering firelight and the last of the sun's rays ignited an anger in his eyes Marnie had never seen before. His lips curled into a sneer. 'You're stalling . . . of course! Something happened all the other times you stupidly decided to do this performance. You are scared!'

Reeling, her hands clutched the copper hair pin against her pounding heart. Notes from a swan's distant call wrapped itself around her like a bear hug. Strength replaced fear.

'YOU had better be scared, Jarrod. You suggested the performance.' Marnie stood on her tippy-toes, pressed the point of the pin level with his chin. 'Whose baby did Zessi have?'

'Mine!' His vocal chords strained. 'All this? Mine. Mine. Mine. Jeeves is my pet project. Tony? Your little friend? Damon's only real successful being. You've seen the dwarves . . . that's how he besieges his guilt! By playing with them. Incidentally, Delray's his gene progeny. Look closely sometime Marnie. You'll see what I mean.'

They turned in the direction of rapidly approaching thundering hooves. Firelight glowed above the riders' heads casting an eerie shadow below.

'Lord Jarrod of Jalekem,' the lead rider called out as they slowed, held out a pair of reins attached to a riderless horse. 'You need to come with us this instant. There is a situation which requires your immediate attention.'

As if commanded by telepathy, Jeeves appeared beside Marnie. 'Lord? What is it you would have me do?'

'Carry on with the show, of course!' he roared and swiftly mounted his ride and turned to gallop away.

'One moment!' Marnie shouted, the hair pin pointed at her brother's back.

Jeeves wrapped his hand around her forearm. 'Come please.'

'It's okay, Jeeves,' she murmured and removed his hand. To Jarrod, she raised her voice and said, 'Do I presume someone has died if you don't return?'

He swung his horse around so viciously it bucked in retaliation, narrowly missing her and Jeeves. Everyone watched in horror as Jarrod sailed through the air and disappeared into a haystack. Rooted to the spot in horror, nobody moved until Marnie started to giggle, looked down at the hair pin and swiftly clipped back her hair. The solemn horse whinnied and nuzzled through the feed. Panicked horsemen followed suit until eventually the stack was almost levelled by the time they helped their

Lord sit upright. Jeeves raced over, waved his arms over Jarrod's body reading out the digital displays that appeared out of nowhere.

'Everything appears to be fine, Lord.'

'Except my pride,' he muttered.

In a louder voice commanded his men to help him stand. He got his balance, tested a few steps and made a beeline towards Marnie.

'Best you go ahead and entertain my people,' he hissed. 'See you later on.'

Her lips twitched mockingly, 'Is that a threat or a promise?'

'Excuse me Lord, but we really need to be somewhere else. Can you ride?' his lead horseman enquired.

Brushing off the helping hands indignantly, Jarrod mounted his horse and trotted off like nothing had happened.

'Jeeves, what is in those pills he keeps popping?'

'Nothing for you, Marnie. Now come along please.'

'I need a moment to myself.'

Jeeves nodded then walked away.

***

Damon and the engineers had tried everything to stabilise the drawbridge. With its broken chain and windlass rendering it useless, new mechanisms were being drafted with orders run back and forth to the forge. Jarrod went ballistic with the threat of the manor being exposed.

'For years, this has been drawn up before sunset. Tonight, of all nights? How could this not have been prevented?'

Nobody dared speak. Instead, made way for the blacksmith lumbering a mass of chain.

'Lord, this one was repaired several year ago.'

'It'll have to do. What do you need?

'Strong men. Oil lamps. Fire,' he grunted.

Meanwhile, by way of the elevated candles Marnie had found her way onto the stage. Through a gap in the curtain sat silently observing her audience devour a mighty feast. She sprung upwards at the sound of a scraping noise behind her.

'Psst, Miss Marnie! It's me, Tony.' His shackled ankles dragged noisily across the dry timber. 'Pops had me stashed in the bridge, we were going to escape . . . but then it wouldn't go up and then Damon found me. He was red with rage and the one who put me in these and threatened to put me on ice. Delray was responsible for putting me in the stable. I crawled from there.'

Aghast, Marnie removed the hair pin and showed him the precious keepsake.

The villagers started chanting, *'Story time! It's story time! Come out and play!'*

'Here, you'll have to do it.'

'But . . . that's the hand forged copper hair pin! It's cursed!'

She had to raise her voice to be heard. 'It is not! Now work it out because I've got a story to tell. You'll know when to run.'

'What about you?' he yelled.

'If it's safe, get to my room and grab my handbag, then meet me at your reading nook. We'll escape from there.'

'We?'

'Isn't that what you were going to do with Jeeves?'

'Um. . . er. . .no, I fibbed.'

Bewildered, Marnie threw her hands up in the air. 'In any case, if something happens to me, RUN AWAY as fast as you can.'

By now, the villagers had started beating the tables with their tankards. The children screeched their impatience.

Marnie held a candle aloft and pushed through the curtains. Her presence, a quietening tonic. A dilapidated desk sat off-centre with an old dining chair at the ready. Very cleverly, a piece of dowel supported a leaning piece of timber.

'Good evening, ladies, gentlemen, boys and girls. Let me begin the tale of *The Mystical Hand Forged Copper Hair Pin.'*

'Halt!' a middle-aged woman stood up. Guards stood around her with open flamed torches. She smiled the second most beautiful real smile Marnie had ever seen.

The actress burst into her role. 'Ah! You must be the first daughter of Jalekem's queen of hearts. A real pleasure,' Marnie curtsied deeply.

'Is that really a mantelet you are wearing?'

'Yes, it is.'

'Carry on then.'

Feeling dismissed, Marnie sat down very carefully. In a whimsical voice, drew her audience in until not a sound could be heard. She held a candle to the long painted fake fingernail. Its shadow cast a huge talon against the backdrop. They gasped in awe. They jumped and shrieked when the mock trapdoor fell loudly onto the hollow stage. Marnie paused, just long enough for them to settle when several horsemen thundered past. The audience stood to see what was causing the disruption and parted as their Lord on horseback pranced through.

His voice clipped. 'Don't let me stop the entertainment. Everything is as it should be.' Jarrod bowed gracefully and once clear of the audience, galloped away.

Marnie lost momentum. She couldn't remember the story. She put her head in her hands. She wished Zessi were there to tell her their story.

***

Damon's sobs turned into anger as he watched the last of his playthings disintegrate in front of his very eyes. It was all Jarrod's fault. *He* did this. *He* was going to pay. Stomping along the canisters, Damon said his goodbyes to the occupants. They were all going to die. Every single one of them. He opened the serving window. Twenty-six Zessi-robots turned and smiled at him. They called his name. They sang to him. They told him how much they loved him.

Projected onto the blackened wall, memorised images of Zessi and him watching another embryo develop, made him smile. It broadened then with a slideshow of Delray as a little baby, then a boy playing on a shuttle-plank, and finally as a lad recording DNA geneology results. The robots made him wipe happy tears. They made him step into their room. They took turns in hugging him, feeling his thinning hair, wrinkles and withered hands. They enticed him to lie down on the bench. They passed a nurse's hat with ebony wig along the production line. The last Zessi-robot gently put it on his head. Damon gazed into the pools of live circuitry as it lowered its face towards his. He didn't feel the needle going into his temple. He didn't know the lights had been turned off. He didn't feel the earth tremble.

***

The cacophony of screams, clanging bells and blasted whistles drowned out Marnie's wails of *fire, fire, fire* as she recited the story and stumbled with the candle into the curtain. With it alight, embers combined with dripping wax set the stage on fire. She prayed Tony had got away. She prayed even harder she could rid herself of the bulky mantelet. Heat penetrated her back. She fell from the second last step, landing face-first into the dirt, winded herself from the books not cushioning her fall. Spot fires hissed and spat at her. The hay stacks sizzled. Her father's voice boomed in her ears. *IT ALL ENDS WITH YOU.* Arguing with herself as she crawled towards the moat; the perils of deactivating the life-support systems extending from the generator room. She would actually be murdering people. She entertained them. Not murdered them. *So, Dad, how does it all end with me?* Her feet were burning. She looked over her shoulder and screamed at the fiery trail catching up to her.

All around her, people were running buckets of water towards the village. Nobody stopped to help her. Nobody stomped on her or even tripped over her. Was she even there? Was she still alive? Was she astral travelling and looking down on her dying body? Was this how it all ended?

Dogs charged past her and leapt into the moat. Children followed suit. Suddenly, she was scooped up and thrown over someone's shoulder. Her head hung by the hipbone of a storm-trooper's leg.

'Jeeves!' she wailed.

*Hope you can swim!* was all she heard as water filled her scream-frozen face.

***

Jarrod barricaded the drawbridge with six of his guards baring jousting poles, shields and swords. Livid at not being prepared for an attack, he behaved like a rabid fox.

'Who controls access to my storey?' he bellowed.

'You do, Lord,' came the unified response.

'Who else?'

'Damon, Lord.'

'Where is he?'

'Nobody has seen him, Lord.'

'We shall defend Jalekem with our lives!' he commanded.

'Yes, Lord. We will do our best.'

'No! We will do so with our lives.'

A series of loud explosions buffeted the air. Three horsemen swept in, their mounts rearing up as bits slammed against their gums.

'Lord! Lord! It's the distillery,' the lead horseman yelled. 'It's gone! We're not being attacked. But we need more helping hands. Homes are on fire. The children!'

'My dogs! Where are my dogs?'

'In the moat!' the rider yelled and galloped off, the other guards hot on his tail.

'Where's my horse?' Jarrod cried. 'Where is my horse?'

Nobody answered. He popped another two tablets, cussed Marnie loudly and began to climb the footholds chiselled into the bridge tower. Half way up, he remembered the pivotal aspect of Jalekem's future. In his haste to descend, Jarrod slipped and landed on the ground with a sickening thud.

***

Utterly exhausted, Jeeves searched for Tony. He hoped he hadn't left it too late to tell the boy the truth. Jeeves swam past where the stable once stood, found the children huddled beside the swan ponds and where Delray swore black and blue he'd seen the boy near the manor.

After instructing the children to stay together, he called for the dogs and commanded them to *stay*.

'I'll help you look for Tony,' Delray told Jeeves.

They swam across to the manor side of the moat. 'Wait, I have to drain my leg,' Jeeves muttered. In doing so, he sobbed, believing the only photograph of his beloved daughter and husband would be totally destroyed.

Delray called out softly, 'That lady, the one on stage. Where is she?'

'Hopefully drying out somewhere, if her burdens didn't sink her.'

'Does she know what we do here?'

'Yes. So don't go blaming her for destroying the village. She isn't cursed. That's a tale from a long-forgotten era.'

'The Lord seems to think she is.'

Jeeves reattached his leg, grunted and held is head. 'Speaking of the devil, he needs my help. Can I entrust you to find Tony and help him if he needs it.'

'Yes, of course, Jeeves! I like him.' Delray waited until he was alone and spoke again. 'And I bet he doesn't know he comes from that donor friend of the Lord Jarrod.'

***

Tony didn't know what to do. He could hear Lord Jarrod moaning and groaning. It was wrong to just leave him. It was wrong to stay at Jalekem. He didn't want to become an experiment, or hang upside down like a bat in sticky liquid until somebody thought it was the right time to make him alive again. He sure as the heck didn't want to be strapped to a board while he was alive neither. He felt awkward around the first queen of heart robots.

'Hah! Got you!' Delray said and gripped Tony's shoulder.

'Please, please let me go. I don't want to be here anymore. They're creating freaks and making babies with one donor, it's so wrong,' Tony whimpered.

'No, you're wrong. They have been using more than one donor, but they need younger donors now. We're almost of age. Jeeves will never get old. We can do this. You and me!'

'Is that why you let me go?'

'Of course! I'm not a cruel basket case, nor will I become one.' Delray lowered his voice. 'Look, over there. I bet that's Jeeves with a real torch! We should move closer.'

The lads dashed across the open grasslands and slid under the nearby bordering shrubs like pro baseball players aiming for first base.

Jarrod's moaning got louder. 'Someone! Help me!'

'We're here,' said Jeeves and dismounted. 'I found your horse minus her saddle. She must have got spooked.'

'I can't feel my legs.'

'You won't feel this then.' Jeeves strapped the dead limbs together and draped Jarrod over the back of his horse.

'He's so strong,' whispered Delray.

'My Pops is the best,' Tony whispered back.

Jeeves spoke loudly. 'The fires are out, nobody got hurt, the dogs are with the children and the mess is being cleaned up. Damon's dead I'm afraid. Futuristically, the Zessi-robots are one option.'

'He knows we're here,' Tony whispered.

Delray stood up dragging Tony with him. 'Actually, Lord Jarrod, Tony and I are your only real option. Before you lose consciousness, how would you like to proceed?'

Jarrod lifted his head. Jeeves shone the torch onto the man's ashen face.

'Save Jalekem,' was all he managed to mumble before his head lolled against the horse's abdomen.

Delray took the reins. 'I know where to take him Jeeves, I believe you and Tony need to discuss a few things.'

'Before you go, young man, I am sorry about Damon.'

'Yeah, sorry for your loss, Delray,' Tony murmured.

The lad sucked in his bottom lip and sniffed hard. After nodding his head several times, he managed to speak. 'It's the right way for life to go, not like your loss Jeeves . . . which reminds me, there's a photo album in the library which belongs to you.'

He turned and led the horse towards the manor.

Tony burst into tears. 'Pops, I panicked. I lost the hair pin, I didn't get Miss Marnie's bag, I just ran away. I hid.'

Jeeves rested his hand on the lad's shoulder and squeezed. He lit up his face, winked then directed the torchlight towards the entrance of the gatehouse threshold.

'You can come out now,' Jeeves called gently.

Wrapped in an oversized towel, Marnie shuffled out. Tony raced over and threw his arms about her.

'I let you down . . .'

'No, you didn't. And it's not right I take you away from here. This really is your home.'

He crossed his arms and pulled himself up to his full height. 'It's yours too, remember! With the beasts incapacitated, you can stay! They can't harm anyone anymore.'

Marnie looked at Jeeves, 'What's going to happen with Jarrod?'

'He'll be wheelchair bound, and duly accommodated in his own suite until his natural demise.'

'I'm fine with that.'

'The gorget is empty,' Jeeves blurted out.

Stunned, Marnie's eyebrows reached for the ceiling of stars. Quickly sensing Jeeves' embarrassment, she said, 'He's the one who should have been on stage!'

Tony tucked a sodden curl away from Marnie's eye. 'Won't you be lonely in Venice?'

'I miss it, Tony. It's where my heart is. That's where my beloved Valentino came from.'

'But his memory can live on here! Hear me out, please Miss Marnie. I've been working on a virtual escape that transports you to wherever you want to go, simply by using the images in your mind. Still a prototype, because I haven't met anybody who has travelled the world before that was prepared to talk to me. You would be the perfect partner, Miss Marnie. Please?'

'What about the smells, the vista, the snow, the humidity, the magnificent architecture, the paintings, the everything else that we don't have here?'

'We create them! We'll be able to bring imagination to life, safely, ethically, all without leaving your favourite seat.'

The lad's beguiling smile enticed the lines of Marnie's mouth to curve upwards. 'Best you go and see what your other partner is up to, young man!'

Tony took off like a shot.

Jeeves clicked off the torch and tucked Marnie's hand in the crook of his arm, gently encouraging her to walk towards the manor. 'Tonight isn't the night for everything to come out into the open, although I am inclined to agree with Tony. Consider staying and being a part of Jalekem's future in any way you see fit.'

'Did you know he was into . . . '

'Exploring the mind's capabilities? Yes! I doubt the world out there are even using ten per cent of their brain these days. In this Land, sure the children have access to the latest fandangle devices, yet they have terrific hand-eye coordination skills and good discipline in a variety of sports. They all know how to ride bikes, horses, sow and reap crops, take out the rubbish and pull their weight with chores. They're polite, respect their elders and can still enjoy childhood.' He vehemently declared, 'Nobody is suppressed. That's one thing I will give credit where it's due. Jarrod was a very fair man when it came to governing principles. The adults have freedom, and this side of the bridge is home.'

'Like a hippy commune?'

'All-in weed and sex? No . . . well, not that I've been invited to anyway!'

They shared a chuckle and walked in silence for a long while.

'What happened to the burdens you wore?' Jeeves asked quietly.

'Resting in the bottom of the moat with Grandad's spirit.'

Jeeves held her while she wept softly.

'I'm okay, thanks Jeeves, but I do think the music room should be utilised more.'

'How about that you take on that responsibility?' he suggested and helped her up the stairs into the grand entrance.

A long-buried quiver of excitement travelled up her spine, squeezed her shoulders and forced a loud sigh out of her mouth.

'Nervous?' Jeeves asked.

'No, quite the contrary,' Marnie said. 'I shall take my leave now. A lavender filled bath is calling my name . . . oh! And so is a plate of roast pork!'

She was about to turn towards the elevators, when Jeeves coughed politely.

'What shall I do with this then?' he asked and held out the copper hair pin.

With regal wave and plum-in-her-mouth accent, Marnie replied, 'Oh, stick it in the gorget!'

**The End**

www.ingramcontent.com/pod-product-compliance
Lightning Source LLC
Chambersburg PA
CBHW010357310726
48979CB00006B/1068

* 9 7 8 1 7 6 3 8 1 4 5 1 6 *